BY SYLVIA ASHTON-WARNER

GREENSTONE

BELL CALL

TEACHER

INCENSE TO IDOLS

SPINSTER

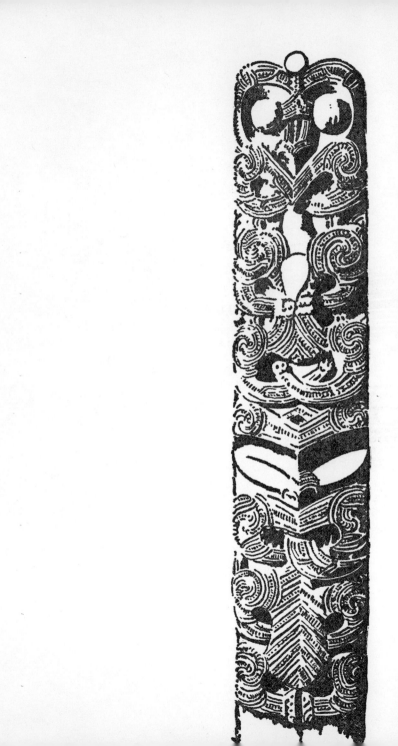

SYLVIA ASHTON-WARNER

GREENSTONE

SIMON AND SCHUSTER • NEW YORK

FIRST PRINTING

LIBRARY OF CONGRESS CATALOG CARD NUMBER: 66-11061
MANUFACTURED IN THE UNITED STATES OF AMERICA
BY H. WOLFF BOOK MFG CO., INC., N.Y.
DESIGNED BY EDITH FOWLER

To
The Whanganui River
New Zealand

A glossary of Maori words appears on page 215.

By the side of a murmuring stream
An elegant gentleman sat.
On the top of his head was his wig,
On the top of his wig was his hat,
On the top of his wig was his hat, hat, hat,
On the top of his wig was his *hat*.

—Old English rune

THE whare sits in the clearing among its ghosts and rains, memories of passions and Maori curses and showers of midsummer. Vivid red and white foxgloves radiate to the circumference of the forest, among them an occasional lost tree fern and many a burnt-out stump. And logs lie about like reproachful corpses telling tales of the past on the slaughter of living native trees by "our civilized brother, the white man."

It may have had a coat of paint one time way back in the former century when some young mill hand had been moved to build it with hope for the future in his brush and a soft new wife in mind, but there's not a sign of it now in its worn colorlessness. To look at, the timber is much like the stumps and plainly related to them, while the iron of the roof is disguised with leaves. So grown into the clearing is the whare as to be of it rather than in it. It could well be growing here like anything else. By one of the windows an ancient tree embraces the whole thing.

Yet there are signs of life. From the edge of the surrounding forest a track leads down through the foxgloves to the back door where a porch opens upon a heavily lived-in kitchen. Except for a sack on the hearth there's no covering on the floor, indeed in the bare boards there is even a hole, not big but still a hole. The walls are bare timber too. So is the table on the inner wall, a long large exhibit to seat a dozen or more, with a form behind and a few chairs around. Nearby a dresser holds stacked dishes.

On the outer wall with the window there's a tough old grand, a small piano that has seen a bit of life, and on the same wall in the far corner behind the door is an iron single bedstead, something else with an obvious history. There is an upturned box beside it on which are lying tidily together a book, a pipe and a tin of tobacco. Just within the back door is the stove, wood projecting from the firebox, and there's a kitchen chair beside it.

Mr. Considine sits on this chair by the stove although it is high midsummer, being a man who finds it hard to keep warm. However, it is late afternoon and in this valley between the ranges the shadows come down early, I assure you; and the breath of the river rises to meet them so that it is not only he who registers the chill of an evening in This Side.

14

The villagers themselves do, the tourists at This Side House in the season and Humpty in the store. As for returning from a cruise on the river with Togi late in the day, you know all about it then. It's a matter of pulling the collar of your coat right up round your face and sharing someone's rug. No, it's not surprising to find him sitting by the stove, especially a man who cannot walk; on each side of his chair leans a crutch.

He's a man in his forties, Mr. Considine, but his face has an agelessness—a delicate face from an in-door life. The black curly hair uncut for some time accentuates the paleness as also does a fair mustache, untrimmed too and flowing. It's a strange thing, I agree, how some men manage to combine dark hair with a fair mustache, and such is the case here. I my-self remember it clearly; besides there hangs a colored portrait of him over the piano in Great-grandma's cottage—or there did until just recently.

He has one of these aquiline turned-down noses you find in the aristocracy, while behind his glasses his eyes can only be described as English blue. Possi-bly the term "English" can account for the whole im-pression; his face has the fine complexion and coloring often bred in the English climate, a fresh but fragile face.

But look at his locked body. Rheumatoid arthritis as we know it but according to the Maoris in the valley it is the "limb-withering" curse of the tohunga makutu.

15

Yet to the younger half of the family, having been brought up with it, it seems all right. To them it is the right way for a father to be and they would not have it any other way. I think that if ever he stood upright one morning before them and walked, as he is always promising he will, it would be the stone end of them. They never question the sharp knees locked in angles —severe right angles they are—after all, they can hold the baby. Or the comically knotted hands: these hands make their porridge however shivering the morning, comb their hair for school, parting it and tying it with string; they hold a pointer to teach them music, put wood on the fire provided there is some, pour a cup of tea for Mumma, and above all, in the evening, brown the potatoes.

He is locked at the hips too so that his whole thin body is a zigzag drawing of what a man's body should be, but you only see this when he gets up on his crutches, a far from graceful performance.

No collar to his shirt and no top button and none on his coat either, which could have belonged to the eldest son, Daniel, who is a very broad young man. Cuffs frayed, of course, reaching too far over his hands and wide gaping pockets with a handkerchief in one and a fair-sized book in the other. And he wears trousers of some faded striped serge too big for him, and he could have been born in these slippers. They're not worn in the parts where slippers usually are but have holes in unlikely places where his feet drag after his crutches. Mrs. Considine must have bought him the slippers at one time or another but no one can say they remember it. He cannot physically have been born in these slippers though he claimed he had once, in a story. Never mind . . . in spite of all this his clothes are at least of himself, harmoniously so, actively, astonishingly promoting an inner elegance. All told, but for his face, he is not unlike one of these comical dwarfs that decorate and electrify his stories.

Richmond D. Considine, Esquire, once a celebrity in the outside world where celebrity seems to matter, sits at the stove in the whare, one sharp knee crossed upon the other, smoothing and browning the potatoes in the pan, his twisted hand cunningly controlling the knife. His back is erect, his head too. Elegance and frailty make up the picture of the man at the stove in the timbered crude kitchen: frailty, elegance . . . mystery.

THE rain steps on the roof like a stealthy thief, so very softly, creating an air of supense in the room, but there is no other sound except the sparking of the fire and the voice of the river until from the distance there's a suggestion of a child crying and you hear, "Mumma, wait for me—ee . . ." Puppa looks up, alerted, the knife poised in his hand. Then another and softer crying in another voice and a second version of "Wait for me—ee."

He clears his throat with portent as though at the beginning of a significant story and with both hands pushes the heavy kettle above the flame. Then Mumma enters the porch laden with parcels and bags, with a sway in her walk as though hitching the weight of her load along. She's a short woman in her late thirties, her body broadening downward to the bottom of her long tweed skirt, and her toes turn out so that her shoes are worn on the outside soles. As she sways doggedly into the kitchen it is plain that although there's little of grace in her there's a vast amount of very much else. Her mouth is lined in determination and feeling burns up the weariness in her eyes. You get a sense of indestructible vitality.

She pauses mid-kitchen, then, hurling her load on the table, dashes to the window and throws it open. "Oh, fresh air, fresh air. You've got no fresh air, Richie." She breathes several deep lungfuls of it before she returns to the table and sinks on the chair there, one arm prostrate before her. She doesn't look at Richmond but out through the window upon the clearing and across the wet foxgloves. Softly, "Well there y'are, y'see."

18

"What is it this time?"

Her palms turn upward. "He let me have the food."

"I'll make you some tea. A cup of tea." He begins on the exercise of getting up and reaches for one of his crutches. "You're tired." Neither mentions she is wet too. Everyone is wet in This Side as a rule.

"It's my head."

"Tea. The answer to everything."

"And my feet too." Sigh. "Standing all day in school." Then with satisfaction, victory, "Anyway I've got the food."

Using one crutch he brings a cup from the dresser to the table.

"Food—an excellent word."

"The skunk." This means Mr. Dunn, owner of the store.

Puppa sets out on the return journey for a saucer. "Exactly. Another fine word. I smell him quite plainly from here. That's why I keep the window shut."

With fire and a lift of the head, "He tried to refuse me the food, Richie, but I threatened him with the p'lice. Starving the whole family, the scoundrel. *Humpty* would have given me the food if that Dunn hadn't been there. *Humpty* knows better than to starve a family. *He'd* give food to a poor mother trying to keep her children alive."

"By God if I could walk . . ."

A snivelly little boy comes in the door, about five,

trousers hanging below the knees and bawling with every enjoyment. But the English beauty still gets through: Puppa's curly black hair shining with raindrops and the dream-blue eyes. "Mumma wouldn't wait for me—ee. . . ."

By now there are two cups and two saucers on the table and a large enamel jug of fresh milk which Mumma has milked from the cow before school, and Puppa, supporting himself on one crutch, sets about putting tea in the teapot. Then, since he can't lift the kettle, "Mary, if you'll just pour the water in the pot."

"I gave him once round." She sweeps back her wet hair with a forearm and sniffs bravely. Her shoulders are wet too and there is mud on her shoes. "I threatened him with the p'lice, the skunk."

"But is that fair to the police?"

Back goes her head in staccato laughter. Just so does the sun follow the rain in the valley of This Side.

A smaller boy appears in the door, a replica of the first, complete with low-slung trousers and high-slung bawling. He's wringing wet too, with muddied bare feet. "Mumma, you wouldn't wait for me—ee. . . ." There are two of them now howling heartily, but no one suggests they stop, their wailing an excellent obbligato to Mumma's laughter. At length she surveys her parcels and bags and sniffs with victory. "Ha-ha, ha-ha, I beat him today." Then with a sudden sigh she lifts her weight from the chair and sways across the kitchen to fill the pot as though still heaving her burdens along.

Puppa is back in his chair by the stove, and, summoning a ready-for-anything voice, "Did anyone see the baby outside?"

"I want a drink," roars the elder boy, Trelawny.

"I 'ant a d'ink," echoes Simon.

Mumma hastily pours a drink for Trelawny, who for some reason is near to her heart, although it is Simon who looks like her. To this day Trelawny remains the one near to her though there was little tangible he could show over the years to have earned it until just recently. ("He looks like Puppa," Great-grandma Considine observes these days whenever Trelawny is mentioned.) Then she gives Simon a drink.

"Trelawny," says Puppa with authority, "go and look for the baby. She might be asleep in one of the rooms."

"I'm too tired. Make Simon go. He's not doing anything."

"Simon, find the baby."

"I'n too ti'ed. Make T'awny go. He not doing an'ing."

"Trelawny, obey me. Find Huia."

"When I've finished being tired."

Mumma consumes her tea audibly, then cuts the boys a piece of bread and butter each, strategically sprinkled with sugar. "Well, I'd better start on the wood before I do the cow. The others should be home to do their practice." Her voice takes on a tone of respect. "Trelawny, will you get the cow?"

"No." Flat.

"Simon, you'll get the cow, won't you?"

"No."

"Richie, Richie, d'you see this? They won't get the cow."

"By God, if I could walk I'd make them get the cow."

Voice rising, "They defy me, Richie, they defy me. And me a trained teacher. They won't help their poor mother who stands on her two feet in a schoolroom all day, and milks the cow morning and night, and drags up the wood from the riverbank and chops it for them, and does the washing and teaches them music and carries home all the parcels and brings up a family of nine singlehanded. I'm as like as not to break every bone in their bodies."

An artistic howl from Trelawny.

"Stop that whining, you little fiend, or I'll give you something to whine *for*."

But Puppa gets back to his point. "Did anyone see the baby outside? She's taken to wandering lately."

"The less I see of that brown rat the better."

"How dare you insult Daniel's daughter with the . . ."

22

"Huh—daughter."

". . . with the Considine blood in her."

"D'you expect me, a trained teacher, t'recognize a dirty little Maori? D'you expect me, a respectable woman, t'bow and scrape to a savage? Even Daniel knew better than to marry the mother. Ha-ha-a . . . *he* knew. Besides, haven't I got enough t'do and enough mouths t'feed without harboring the illegitimate?"

Puppa is trembling with rage. "Trelawny," he roars, "find Huia."

"No."

"God damn it, Simon, find the baby."

"No."

"By God, if I could walk." He fumbles passionately for his crutches, struggles to his feet and swings agitato through the other three rooms. Returning, "God 'pon m'soul, will no one in this house obey me? Am I not head of this house? Do *I*, a cripple, have to find the child?" He moves in swift jerks toward the door. "O God give me back the use of my legs. O God why must I endure this infirmity? O God release me from this hell. O God have mercy on me."

"Well, I'd better change and get the wood." Mumma sniffs with indifference and rises.

The two small boys follow Puppa with interest as he struggles dangerously down the outside step—he's supposed to have help getting down this step. No longer feeling too tired apparently, the boys trail one behind the other after him, winding up the track behind him through the listening foxgloves, on occasion ducking ahead of him to remove some stick from his way. Every few steps Puppa rests on his crutches, lifts his head and his voice and calls in a trembling falsetto, "Cooee! Cooee! Hu—ia! Hu—ia!"

The rain has passed by for a moment and the late afternoon sun licks at the drops, while all around towers the forest, listening, thinking, recording the scene. More steps, more calls, "Hu—ia! Hu—ia!" until Puppa and his followers disappear at the end of the track where it links with the down-river lane, and all there is left at the whare in the clearing is a lone short woman with hair in her eyes doggedly chopping wood.

A few showers later a group of children, their arms full of fungus, wind their way out from the forest and pause at the end of the track, two girls and a boy. Someone has lightly told them, or they have made it up themselves, that fungus will sell in the outside world, and they plan to buy a wheelchair for Puppa. Flower, about nine, with brown curls to the shoulders and the loveliest wide green eyes and as many freckles on her face as there are foxgloves in the clearing, is known as the "flower o' the flock." It was either Puppa or Mumma who supplied the title and Flower is the last to dispute it. She says, "Look, I'm going to hide mine away here," and stuffs her fungus under a fern.

Susanna is the next, insignificant looking. Her hair is mercilessly plaited and tied at the back with string. Strags fall over her face by now since Puppa did her hair this morning, and she goes in for freckles too. If you study her face closely enough you'll see Puppa's features, but I don't think anyone has, although you do hear at times, "She's got Puppa's nose."

"Me too," she echoes and hides hers too.

The boy is Lance. Like Hamish out in the world, Lance prefers his feet soundly on the ground and says he's going to be a scientist, although no one has ever seen him absent himself from Puppa's stories in the evening, streams of extraordinary fantasy. Mumma has given her face to Lance, her firm no-nonsense features, which actually poor Sue could have done with, failing something more obvious from Puppa.

"Me too," he agrees with Flower.

All have faded but clean clothes, at least they were clean this morning when they left for school, a little too long below the knee, bare feet all round, and their hair is falling over their eyes, even Flower's curls which are tied with a bright green ribbon given to her by one of the older girls out in the world, Rose, I believe. All three have this romantic waiflike appearance that comes to children of a forest.

Flower straightens anxiously. "Mumma's home. I can hear the ax. We shouldn't have left Puppa so long." Her green eyes observe the whare down the

25

track. As she gazes she changes, surveying the sea of foxgloves, and draws herself erect and speaks with excitement. "Look at me. I'm a famous dancer. See all that?" indicating the foxgloves. "That's all the people in the audience and this path is the stage. Watch me." Up lift her arms and her toes too and here is a graceful fantasia, until she pauses and bows. "Hear the people clapping?"

"Me too," from Sue.

"Me too," from Lance, and the next thing here is a line of one-two-three as they whirl and dip down the path through the red and white blooms, secret yellow buttercups and starfaced daisies, and as they dance the rain returns, a feathery unreal version, blurring the outlines of the children like a camera intentionally off-focus or like a shaded spotlight, until they arrive at the back door of the house and push puffing and dripping through the porch. A moment they listen, then enter the kitchen.

But Puppa is not sitting at the stove browning the potatoes for tea with the baby on his knee, which is really a terrible thing. A piece of wood has fallen to the hearth and the kettle is no longer hissing. For a moment they stare, then each scatters to the other three rooms only to return unspeaking. Now, in one mind still, they run through the front room and out that door where the flowers and grass are worn to the soil by many feet, and there a few yards off is

Mumma, by now milking the cow, sitting with her face tucked in Lily's flank and a coat over her shoulders.

"Where's Puppa?" from Flower.

"Gone." She sniffs off responsibility and goes on milking, the only sound in the clearing the squirt-squirt of milk frothing in the bucket, a remark from the tui in a tree, a reflective remark yet with a question in it, and of course the voice of the river rumbling over her rapids.

"Where are the kids?" from Lance.

Fiercely, lifting her head, "Don't say 'kids,' say 'children.' "

"Where are the children then?"

"You should never use slang in my presence."

"Did you have a row with Mr. Dunn?" from Sue.

Mumma spits in the dust and leaves it.

Once more in common mind they wheel and set off in the favorite formation in the clearing, one after the other like birds in flight—the biggest first, next biggest following, trailing off to the youngest at the end, back along the path they have come, no longer performing on an imaginary stage but living their own rich drama. When the path reaches the forest it turns, descends and widens to a lane which follows the bank of the river.

They seem to know exactly where to go, these three bush wraiths, trotting in and out of the trees with the light ease of other forest creatures, ducking the over-head branches, skipping reared roots until, sure enough, not very far along where the lane swings near the water at a place called "Puppa's corner," here is Puppa himself sitting on a too-low log and gazing upon the water, his crutches tidily beside him. Simon is sitting near on the same log copying him exactly, knees crossed, one hand upon the other, even to a pair of sticks for crutches also tidily beside him, and Trelawny is swinging on a branch above, the foliage flicking Puppa's ear.

The flowing mustache with raindrops upon it quivers when he sees the children and two tears appear. "Confound it," he breathes. "God damn it."

"Are you here?" from Flower.

"God 'pon m'soul."

"Where's Huia?" from Flower.

"Where's the baby?" from Sue.

"Are you looking for Huia?" from Lance.

A burst of irritation. "Stop that infernal boy crashing at my eardrum with that infernal branch—" the quivering stops and the tears retreat—"before I lose my reason." Adds, "And my hearing too."

"Stop that, you little wretch," from Lance.

"Shut up," from the tree.

"I'll give you a jolly good hiding."

"Shut up, shut up, shut up."

"All right, I'll climb up and box your ears."

A pathetic wail from the tree. "I'll tell Mumma on you—oo . . ." But the flicking stops.

Flower says, "You wait here, little Puppa, and we'll find Huia."

"Me too."

"Me too."

Puppa clears his throat with portent as though opening an astounding story: "Captain Togi should be informed with no loss of time that Huia Brice Considine, princess of the ngati Te Renga Renga and future paramount chieftainness of the river tribes, has been missing for over two hours." The children are at once enthralled and with no preparation at all swing into their roles. Even Trelawny lets up on his bawling. With Puppa about it's quite impossible to distinguish the real from what's not.

"I'll fly and tell Togi," from Sue.

"I'll remain with my father and defend him," from Lance.

"I will search and search," from the flower o' the flock. The thing about Flower that so draws everyone is her inheritance from Puppa of so large a quota of his habitual drama, not to mention his instinct for audience. She lifts her head, tosses back her curls, and her green eyes widen with light. "I'll search the clearing, search the river and search the whole of the forest. I'll search, search, search and search until I discover the princess."

Again the children are entranced and Puppa is too. For the moment the line between reality and fantasy has escaped them all. Currently no one knows whether Huia is actually lost or not, unless it is Lance again, who likes the security of the ground; he is disposed to keep hold of events as they *are* to be sure where he is. "Go on, Sue, then, and let Togi know. Go on, Flow, you go and search. I'll take Puppa home." With discomfort the other children make the difficult transition from fantasy down to earth and Trelawny resumes his bawling.

"Hurry up, you two," from Lance, "it might start to get dark soon." And off dash Flower and Susanna in opposite directions; Flower back up the lane the way they had come and Sue down the lane to This Side landing where Togi ties up his boats.

"Confound it, I'm cold," from Puppa.

"I want to go home," whines Trelawny.

"I 'ant to go home," copies Simon.

"Oh shut up, you two," from Lance.

Togi of course knows exactly where to find the next rangatira of the ngati Te Renga Renga and heir to all its lands. He brought Huia on his back only last Sunday to the lost meeting house for an outing and a break from the other Considines. After he had delivered his guests from a cruise up-river he made straight for little Huia. He'd always meant to bring her here where her parents had been so happy. Returned at last from the First World War, he keeps both eyes on Huia.

It was here in this deserted meeting house that Huia was conceived. Not that anyone could be sure of this, there being any amount of conceiving places in the valley of This Side, especially in the spring and summer; and Daniel with Huia's mother, Kaa, certainly used them all, but most of the time they were here.

As Togi makes his unerring way along the forgotten track, weaving like a tunnel through massive trunks overlaid with delicate creeper and between the frothing ground ferns, Flower and Sue trail him. More nervously however they follow him as he steps upon the veranda of this haunted place, lowers his head for the Maori door opening and penetrates the odorous gloom. And sure enough, just as in one of Puppa's stories, here they find Huia sleeping, tucked in a ball like a forest creature all but covered in hair. You can see little more beyond the hair than two bare feet.

"Jus' like I think, ay?" as he picks the child up. "I think when I bring her here las' Sunday, now this kid she's going to come back here on her lonesome and get herself los' and have everybody flying about. An' now here she is. You come here on your lonesome, Huia? Jus' what I think las' Sunday."

On Sundays, occupied with his smart guests from This Side House, you'll find Togi in his captain's uniform with this lovely cap, creased trousers, pressed tie and the whitest shirt on the river, but today is not Sunday but a working day of the week and a man's working clothes take the place of the captain's glory.

Flower and Sue do not run to the carved panels of the ancestors on the walls with their eerie pauashell eyes; the gloomy atmosphere terrifies them. They remain together, touching each other, surveying with reserve and with no admiration whatever the painted rafters on the tall ceiling, the long ridgepole and the two holding-up posts, all but brushing off physically the spirits of the ancestors crowding invisibly about them.

"Fancy bringing her here," from Sue. "Why did you bring Huia here last Sunday, Togi?"

"Tha's why it's a happy place."

"*This* a happy place? Why?"

"Huia's mother and father they have a love in this place." He wraps his coat round the baby who has wakened in his arms. Her skin is almost as white as Flower's but her hair and her eyes give the Maori blood away. She is a very pretty child with a full top lip and eyes like canoes tethered at an angle. "An' how's my little kid, ay?"

She stretches out an arm the size of a doll's. "My arm it gets bleed, don't they?" There is in fact a scratch on it.

"What's 'have a love' mean?" from Flower.

"Like . . ." pause . . . "kiss and get kissed."

"What for?"

"Like, that's how a baby it gets borned."

"How does a baby get born?"

Togi sets off back through the door opening into the tree light of the enclosure, the two girls keeping close. "Well, like . . . y'see . . . when a man and a woman they have a love, then a baby it might get borned. I learn a word from one of my gues's, 'conceive.' Tha's a good word. This Huia she get conceive here."

"Exactly what does 'conceive' mean?"

"Tha's why a baby it jus' start to get borned."

"But *what* makes it start to get born?" They are on the track again, now following in single file beneath the lofty tree ceiling.

"Jus' what I say, ay. A man and a woman they have a love."

"And won't a baby start to get born if a man and a woman don't have a love?"

"Tha's for sure."

"Won't a man and a man having a love start a baby getting born?"

"I doesn' see how it can."

"Or a woman and a woman?"

"If it does I never heard it."

"But Togi—Puppa and Mumma don't have a love, yet nine of us children so far got borned."

33

Silence in the tree halls but for the whisper of their feet on the crushed fern frond and the touch of the rain on the tall leaf ceiling until Togi says with finality, "Look here, you kids. You talk too much. You sure ask too much question."

Down the lane the damp breath of the river creeps up the banks to meet the descending shadows, and the chill of the forest is on Puppa. All three boys have tried to pull him to his feet and start him off homeward but the log is too low to get up from. They hurt his hands as they tug, and his arms too, and there's a short shout or two of pain. Finally they give it up. Lance takes to drawing wheels on a bank with a stick, Trelawny settles down to some serious bawling and Simon nestles closer to Puppa.

When the others arrive, however, Flower and Sue get him up and give him both his crutches while Togi keeps Huia. Now the trek homeward begins. Flower and Sue walk each side of him, Lance walks ahead kicking the way clear and plotting a dry course through the mud, Flower takes Simon on her back with Trelawny roaring behind. And yet Puppa seems very happy out here in the forest with all the others around him and the river right below, Trelawny giving the area a touch of home—though Puppa calls for more and more stops, and crutches more and more slowly. Even so he tells a minor story about Mr. Dunn, the owner of This Side House, the store, the landing and both the boats on the river, not to mention being chairman of the school committee.

The company hears how Mr. Dunn made mountains of money, real mountains as high as these ranges, all shining gold the lot, and how he stood on the top of this mountain of gold to prove to all that he owned it. But the gleaming coins were loose and shiny and the Dunn began a-slipping. The slipping grew to a skidding and the skidding grew to a mighty slithering as down from the mountain the Dunn came skithering to be buried in the coins at the bottom. "Wealth," he sums up, "is destructive whereas poverty can be creative."

"C'eatif," from Huia.

But it is hard getting him up the rise where wet clay is as slippery as golden coins. "How did you come so fast before, Puppa?" Flower hands Simon over to Lance since Sue won't carry him, takes the baby from Togi who distributes the crutches and picks Puppa up in his arms as easily as Daniel used to do, so that in time they all reach home.

Togi sets Puppa down within the back door of the porch, fixes his crutches in his armpits and walks off in the darkness. Flower puts the baby down on her feet, too, Lance unloads Simon, and then the six of them, Puppa included, file silently into the kitchen where

Mumma is stoking the fire. They trek in single file the length of the room to Puppa's bed in the corner, and he sits on the side of it. Then the rest of them make for the table with the pan of potatoes there.

And what should Mumma do but make the tea and pour two cups. "Take him his tea, Susanna." She even sits on the black box at the foot of the bed in which are housed Puppa's original manuscripts, his coat of arms and the genealogy of his family, and talks to him calmly as though nothing had happened since she last saw him. She talks about the successes of the older ones battling in the outside world, and nothing enraging whatever. From all of which the children read that for a while at least it will be safe to leave Puppa with Mumma. Not that it matters what they read, since Puppa has a heart attack anyway on his bed behind the door, so that there's no story time tonight.

Heart attacks pass by, however, and the time comes after tea with the dishes done when the children are either settled down round the long table at their homework in the moth-flown lamplight—there's no such thing with Mumma about of having the windows shut—or taking their turns at practicing their music on the piano, violin or flute.

"Mumma," ventures Flower, "what does 'conceive' mean?"

"What's that, what's that?"

"What does 'conceive' mean?"

"Get on with your homework."

"Mumma," risks Susanna from the piano near the door, "how did nine children get born when you and Puppa don't have a love?"

"What's all this? Who have you been playing with? Have you been talking to that common creature Eva Dunn? You get on with your practice."

Puppa stirs on his pillows behind the door and his hands change places. "An angel brings children," he says.

Later, however, Mumma still does her own singing practice at the piano, her roughened hands marvelously manipulating the keys, and the songs are sweet sentimental love songs. In the morning you hear her speaking lines at breakfast from the poetry she teaches at school. "The Arab's Farewell to His Steed," "The Slave's Dream," and such, touched up with a few rare tears. All of which the children love . . . especially the one about "They grew in beauty side by side, They filled one home with glee. Their graves are scattered far and wide, By mount and stream and sea. . . ."

But a night or two later story time resumes, and after their music and homework when the children in their white nightclothes have grouped round Puppa's bed, or on it, grandly both they and he scale the barrier between the real world and that other, not however without a preliminary skirmish.

"Once upon a time . . ."

"Get your feet off me, Lance," from Sue. "Puppa, Lance's foot is touching me."

". . . there was . . ."

"Well, you move away," from Lance. "This is my place, I always sit here."

". . . a forgotten meeting house in the heart of the forest. In this ancient Maori building paneled with the carved images of the ancestors of the race there was . . ."

"Stop it, Lance. I got here first."

"Oh, be quiet. Anyone would think I *wanted* to touch you. As a matter of fact I don't. I prefer my feet on the ground. I heard Puppa telling Mumma."

"God 'pon m'soul."

"Kod pom soul," from Huia in Flower's lap.

From Sue, "Well, I can't stand him touching me. I can't stand anyone touching me." With her tight-plaited hair and anger she looks so ugly.

From Flower, "Lancelot, move your feet away from Susanna. Go on, Puppa, we're good now."

"Go on, Puppa."

"Go on, Puppa."

"Go Puppie," from Huia, at which they all yell with laughter.

An aggrieved clearing of the throat, his knees poke

sharp from under the bedclothes and his hands fold upon them. He lifts the under one and lays it upon the other. "Confound it," with lessening feeling, "I've lost my line of thought."

A tentative silence. The square of darkness from the open window is a highway for anything with legs or wings, and through it drifts the voice of the river bustling over her night rapids and the shriek of a late cuckoo. "Once upon a time . . ." he tests, and waits.

"Once upon a time in the depths of the forest . . ."

"You said 'heart' of the forest last time."

He takes this, it being at least relevant. "Once upon a time in the heart of the forest there was a forgotten meeting house, forgotten by all but the forest spiders and a few indolent birds. Well, there were a few other forest creatures, furred, feathered or haired, who thought it a lovely home. 'An absolute gift,' they said.

"Now you mightn't think so, but one day someone else arrived there looking for a home, not furred, feathered or haired at all. You've no idea who it was. It was a dark-haired princess. She was an astonishingly beautiful princess; her hair was as black as a tui's back with the same iridescent sheen, her face was as white as the thousand-jacket and easily as soft, if not softer, her lips were as red as that puriri blossom growing outside on the tree, and her eyes like deep forest pools. They were liquid and dark, they were deep and still and reflected the mystery about them. As for her

39

royal body it put to shame the rain wraiths that drift the length of the river.

"Yet she was unhappy. She had run away from the palace, she confided to a fantail, because she had not been able to see eye to eye with her stepmother, who as is usual with stepmothers, had committed the unforgivable sin: she was not exactly like the real mother, than which no stepmother makes a graver error. This new mother was dark whereas the first had been fair. Was this not inconsiderate? But we can't all be perfect and stepmothers have much to live up to. We could well be more indulgent to the whole misunderstood class.

"So one day, she told this fantail during his morning break from flirting, grieving for her golden-haired real mother, she ran off into the forest tearing her dress on the nettles and shedding strands of her hair, and, in case this was not sufficient clue to anyone who might follow her, she took care to drop accidentally her dainty handkerchief and also her little prayer book, in obvious places, of course, and even left on an open log her ring with a coronet on it, for what's the good of running away if no one knows where to find you? What an indispensable facet of the art of completely disappearing this leaving of clues is!

"When she finally came upon the forgotten meetinghouse the forest creatures greeted her with reserve. But they did bring her berries and nuts to eat and the birds laid eggs for her. As for the spiders, who caught at once that she was royal, they set to work in teams weaving her a gossamer coronet from their second-best webs. They took shifts on this job, it was so arduous.

"But too much time passed by to suit the princess before anyone came panting after her to beg her to return, and just as she was beginning to worry that she hadn't left enough clues and that perhaps she could see eye to eye with her stepmother after all, what do you think happened?

"Who should arrive at the edge of the forest but a rather nice stranger. Now when other people come to the edge of the forest they simply pass by. Why plow into darkness and brambles? But this stranger had the spirit of curiosity which is the difference between people. He liked to see what none had seen and find what none had found. The mystery of the trees provoked him. Plainly no one else had entered, so taking some bottles of water and bread in a pack he secretly made an entrance.

"Quite soon he came upon a piece of flimsy dress but then nothing else. Each day he struggled in-forest to find whom the dress belonged to but each night returned to base in failure. Many a time there was when he decided to give it up, until one morning when drinking his water he found a strand of hair, at which he suddenly changed his mind. Soon after this he found the handkerchief and in time he found the prayer book, so how could a man give up? He went through a lot more bottles of water during the weeks that followed, and loaves and loaves of bread, and had all sorts of trouble trying to explain away to the villagers his many cuts and scratches, until there came a late afternoon when just as he was sitting resting on a log—an open log it was—he saw the ring gleaming. 'Good gracious me,' he cried, 'is this a ring I see?' He felt he was near. He believed he was near. He sprang to his feet and . . ."

"It's time the children went to bed," through the wall from Mumma, who is in bed herself. "I'll never get through my days if I don't get my rest."

"Oh no, Mumma."

"Go on, Puppa."

But Puppa begins singing softly an old rune that means he has finished for the night.

"By the side of a murmuring stream
An elegant gentleman sat.
On the top of his head was his wig . . ."

"Did the stranger find the princess, Puppa?"

"On the top of his wig was his hat . . ."

"Did the princess like the stranger, Puppa?"

"On the top of his wig was his hat, hat, hat . . ."

"Just tell us quickly, Puppa, did they marry? Just say yes or no."

"On the top of his wig was his *hat*."

· ·

The next night, believe me, there is no time lost in preliminary skirmishing. In record time the dishes are done and homework and music over. No one ever saw them wash their feet so fast and get into their white nightclothes. For Puppa's part, he cooperates. In no time he gets the stranger down a track leading to an enclosure, over the veranda of an exotic building paneled with carved ancestors, the like of which he has never seen, through the low door opening on which he bumps his head and "sure enough here was a princess lying on the earth floor and moaning in an interesting way, cobweb coronet and all. Kneeling beside her,

" 'My princess, I've found you.'

" 'Go away, I'm busy.'

" 'Busy? You don't seem to be.'

" 'I'm busy being ill,' she said.

" 'How extraordinarily interesting. But couldn't you change your occupation? Why not be busy getting well?'

" 'I couldn't think of anything more boring than to be busy getting well.'

" 'But you'd want to get well for *me*,' he said.

" 'No I would not. I'm not interested in men.'

" 'I've never,' he replied, 'met a woman not interested in men. You'll never get married that way.'

" 'I *have* got married that way. Now let me get on with my moaning.'

" 'You *are* married?' he said in despair, for the first time looking about him. 'I see no sign of a husband.'

" 'That's not likely,' she said, 'since I've married somebody invisible.'

" 'Did you say "invisible?" '

" 'You heard me,' she replied.

" 'Tell me, who is this invisible husband? It seems a good idea.'

" 'I happen to have married the god of the forest. His name is Tane Mahuta.'

" 'So that's why you moan, dear princess. This god has been cruel to you.'

" 'Not exactly that. It's just that I never see him except when I am dreaming.'

" 'I agree that that is moaning material of the very highest order. But I'm not without a solution. Allow me to deputize for your husband, the invisible forest god. That is, when you're awake. When you're asleep and dreaming, of course, I'd leave the field to him. In this case I'd prefer to deputize.'

"The princess rose on an elbow and for the first time looked him over. 'You're extremely ugly,' she said.

" 'Not at all, my dear. No one is at his best with half the forest in his hair, all of the forest mud on his boots and acres of flesh torn off. Give me a day or two to repair myself, then take another look. Then you can make your decision.'

" 'I've made it already, stranger. It doesn't matter what you look like, really, since I'll never be in love with you. But the crude physical fact remains that I could do with a mortal stand-in. Or a mortal sleep-in if you like. When I'm not dreaming, that is.'

"The stranger reflected a moment, then he said, 'I expect that the role of a mortal deputy, a stand-in for a woman's dreamings of some perfect god, is the most a husband can count on.'

" 'Think so?' she said. Then as usual, thinking of herself first, 'But will I be happy with you?'

" 'Passably,' he said. 'As happy as anyone can be when they're married. There's always the "eternal beloved." ' "

"Richie, Richie," from the kitchen where Mumma is doing the ironing, "let the children get to bed. They've got their school in the morning." Huia is asleep in Flower's arms, and Simon and Trelawny.

Puppa is silent for some moments and doesn't seem to be able to make the always difficult journey from fantasy back to reality. His hands folded one upon the other change places in agitation until Lance, of all people, begins singing for him in his pure voice.

"By the side of a murmuring stream
An elegant gentleman sat . . ."

"That's a hard story, Puppa," from Flower.

45

Lance says, "What's all that about 'crude physical fact'?"

"On the top of his head was his wig . . ."

"And Puppa," from Flower, "what do you mean by a 'mortal sleep-in'?"

"On the top of his wig was his hat . . ."

"Did she *like* being ill?" from Sue.

"Most women do. On the top of his . . ."

"How could a princess have a love with a god, Puppa, when he was invisible?"

"She couldn't. That's why she needed the mortal stand-in. On the . . ."

"Do you mean the princess will have a love with the stranger and pretend he is the god?"

"That is the usual procedure. On the top of his wig was his hat, hat, hat . . ."

"Have you got an eternal beloved, Puppa?"

"On the top of his wig was his *hat*."

Many months later, dating from round about here, the children cannot help but notice a pile of towel diapers growing on the machine in the front room, and baby clothes too, which they are told are for the Belgians. "Surely you know about the poor little Belgians having a terrible time in the war? We've all got to do our bit."

Behold my paddle!
It is laid by the canoe side,
Held close to the canoe side.
Now it is raised on high, the paddle,
Poised for the plunge, the paddle.
Now we leap forward.

Behold my paddle, Te Roku-o-whiti!
See how it flies and flashes.
It quivers like a bird's wing
This paddle of mine.

Ah, the outward lift and the dashing!
The quick thrust in and the backward sweep;
The swishing, the swirling eddies,
The foaming white wake and the spray
That flies from my paddle!

—Paddle song of the Aotea Canoe
(fourteenth century)

T his Side is a valley in the ranges cut deep in the shape of a heart. These ranges are covered entirely with forest from the slopes to the highest peaks, excepting for the village area which is one wild declaration of flowers. On the floor of the valley flows the river, the ever-running tears at the bottom of a heart, as you hear Mr. Considine say.

On this side of the river is the village of This Side with the House, the store, the school and the pa, the road and the landing and such, but on the far side of the river, which they call *That* Side, there's comparatively little life. Since the big flood three years ago the pa has not wholly recovered: several of the people were drowned that night and there's a tapu on the place; moreover, most of the animals were washed away and the kumara crops covered in silt, inches and inches of it.

But Huia's great-grandfather still lives there, the

rangatira paramount of the river tribes, the ngati Te Renga Renga. Close beneath the tree-dark hills he draws his life out in the Dwelling Place among the spirits of his ancestors; above him the painted rafters, about him the glaring paua-shell eyes of the carving on the walls and before him the changeable river.

He is one of the old-timers of the Maori race, who began to die out early in the century, and is a scholar of the Maori culture. He can recite the list of his chieftain ancestors from a period some eight hundred years ago, long before the historic canoes crossed from Tahiti and other eastern Pacific islands to New Zealand. Several lists, in fact, for there were collateral tables of names down through the generations from the far-back Hawaikian days, and not mere shadowy names, but most of them with some definite tradition attached in the orally preserved history of the tribes. Practically every Maori then, not merely those with claims to high aristocratic descent, could name his forefathers back to the era of the migrations and many could go a few beyond that time.

"This pride of pedigree had a certain value in it. It made often for a chivalrous spirit, a scorn of mean actions. A 'rangatira' would endeavor to behave as his renowned ancestors had behaved in certain circumstances. Of course, like the white man's ancestors, some of those long-gone rangatiras were great ruffians, but there were the outstanding names imperishably associated with deeds of bravery, endurance and generosity."

He was born too far back in the former century to be educated at Te Aute but had been sufficiently taught by an Anglican mission on the Whanganui River to take his place there as one of the teachers much later in life. There he had a hand in schooling young Maoris destined for Pacific renown later in the new century: Ngata, Pomare and Rangi-Hiroa, with ripples of letters after their names and European titles. To a modest extent he was responsible for these "saviors of his people in their extremity when the Maori race, under the impact of the white man, was regarded as doomed in the long run to disappear."

But whereas the younger Maori leaders went out into the field of politics, medicine and law, ranging through other countries in pursuit of perfection in their crafts to bring back to their people, the older Te Renga Renga, who back in the last century would have taken degrees in anthropology and letters, had there been a university at that time, could do no more than sit back among his people and teach from That Side pa.

A knightly soul is Te Renga Renga, chivalrous, kindly and generous in the instinctive manner of a true rangatira. Also intensely patriotic in the Maori sense, as well as broadly imperial in his outlook. No subtribe up-, down- or across-river will forget his elo-

51

quent and impassioned appeals in the days of the recent Great War to keep the Maori Pioneer Battalion up to full strength on the Western front.

His great private curse however is the disposition of the women of his family to die absurdly young. In his most Maori moments he believes in the curse laid upon them by the Tohunga Makutu when Te Renga Renga's only daughter and child, Whai, gave herself to the white Brice Clarendon. "Death by childbirth, death by limb-withering," was the burden of the chant "to avenge Whai Te Renga Renga." Although in his enlightened times he admits it is no more than physical misfortune; his own wife died young before any curse was chanted. "Ah, well," to quote young Humpty at the store, "the graves are full of Te Renga Renga women who never saw this side of childbirth."

As he had neither son, grandson nor great-grandson, a rare thing in a Maori family, all that he is left with is a great-granddaughter in the person of the infinitesimal Huia, who is not even half Maori but only a quarter. Not that he minds this too much; he values the white blood in her since he knows it to be a good one, from young Daniel Considine. Besides, possibly, the preponderant three-quarters of it could well break the Maori curse as well as challenge whatever physical weakness there was in the Te Renga Renga women. But the whole thing remains a hidden sadness running like tears at the bottom of his heart like the river at the bottom of the valley.

All of which, as told in This Side where the villagers do little else than tell one another things over the beer in Mai's big copper, over the counter to Humpty in the store, at the pa after the latest burial of some silly who got himself drowned, or under the linden trees, is the reason why the old one allows this last small remnant of his blood to be brought up with the Considines. Maybe there is something in the white home and in the white blood, missing in his own, which will give the mokopuna endurance, they say, or at least resist the Maori curse. Moreover, everybody knows the rangatira's respect for the cripple in the clearing with whose forgotten fame in the outside world on the other side of the globe he is not unacquainted. As for Humpty, he dismisses the whole subject as thoroughly overworked. "They're too skinny, and that's all there is to it."

Togi often brings Huia across-river by canoe on a late Sunday afternoon if he can unload his guests early enough from a cruise on the river, putting them off at the landing to plod up the flower-lined road to the House. In the summer, that is, when the days are long and when the guests are here. In the winter he brings her earlier. Not that he ventures too near the clearing now that Mrs. Considine is there, but there are all sorts of ways of abducting Huia without putting his foot in it. The children are usually making themselves houses in the trees or gathering fungus there and the baby is often with them. And when they are not he can count on Flower to bring the baby down the lane as far as the corner bridge. Like everyone else, he is fond of Flower, as Huia is too. There he swings Huia on his back, takes her down to the landing, unfastens a dreaming canoe and the next thing they're on the surface of the water on their way to That Side pa.

This afternoon Huia's extravagant black hair is wet and she can barely see through it. Puppa tries to comb this hair but he says he loses his comb in it. Her bare feet are muddied and her dress too long but in her mind all is order. No racial conflict yet assails her when moved from one race to another although she's inclined to hang on to Togi; she sits on his knee, twists, stands, pulls and climbs all over him, enraging to a European but nothing to Captain Togi, as he joins with several young Maoris gathered in That Side pa, for the haka and the poi practices and for a Maori culture lesson.

On occasion she glances at the severe old face of her great-grandfather, her koro, but in curiosity rather than love. He is chanting in elusive quarter-tones in running Maori to the class, but her own time to learn has not yet come.

"O young ones," begins the old one, "attend.

"In this way the beginning,
In this way the creation.
Night and night and night.

Night the first, night the tenth, night the
        hundredth,
Night the many hundredth.
Generations and generations of night.

Night without time,
Night without time,
Night all-enveloping.
Came Papa, the earth.

Lay upon her in great heaviness,
Rangi the sky father.
Lay upon her in never-ending darkness
Rangi the dominating.
Crushed between them in their dark embrace,
Their god family.

Confused and cramped, the god children,
Rebelled they against their imprisonment,
Struggled they to part their parents.

Spoke, at length, one of the god children,
Tane Mahuta, god of the forest:
'Do not slay our parents, O god brothers,
Lift we, rather, our father on high,
Set him there forever above us.'

Began they to separate their parents,
Chanted they as they heaved:
'E iki, e iki e!
Te torou o whiti.
Hiki nuku e.
Hiki rangi e.
Ha . . . ha!
Ka hikitia tona uri!
Ka hapainga uri.
I aa ia.
I aia!' *

Prised they their parents apart,
Forced they their father on high.
Covered Tane his earth mother, Papa,
With his trees and birds
For her clothing and adornment.

When parted thus the parents,
Came Ao the light,
The sun, the moon, the stars,

---

* Ancient authentic lifting chant.

The children of the Supreme One,
Brilliant, suffusing the vast spaces
Bringing wonderful life to the earth.
Clothed Tane his father with stars.

In this way the beginning.
In this way the creation."

E Tane!
I unuhia a nuku,
I unuhia a rangi,
Maunutanga,
Mareretanga,
O tenei tauira,
O tenei ariki!

—Maori karakia

Which means:

O Tane, reveal to me the origin of this evil!
Release the dark curse from this sufferer,
O spirits of the sky.
Let the evil fly from him,
Let it be cast from him,
From the body of this sacred one,
This chief!

Two or three years beat by, maybe four. Time is ill-kept in This Side, chronologically. Only Mr. Dunn can be relied on to know what the date is or how many years have passed, and who's going to ask Mr. Dunn? Better to ask Humpty who knows the date when it suits him, and you may strike a time when it does. For that matter who *wants* to know trivia like a date? Can you eat it or swim in it or sleep with it? Why bother about it then?

As for how many years have passed, all you've got to do according to Humpty who misses nothing whatever, is to note the new babies in any one family. In the clearing, for instance, he recalls registering two, he being the registrar of births and deaths; a boy called Richmond after his father and one called Clarendon, a girl, named, if you must know, after the very young man who first brought down the curse on the clearing, Brice Clarendon, an Englishman, way back at the beginning of the century when he seduced Whai Te Renga Renga, the old one's daughter.

Whai? There she is up on a hill under a poplar. Where else would she be? No, he didn't marry her though he wanted to. The Tohunga Makutu wouldn't let him, tossing off one curse after another on the clearing where they did their loving. So that all that young Brice Clarendon left behind him was of course a baby and a wonderful ring bearing the Clarendon coat of arms, which is to be seen any time on the finger of no less than our boatman, Togi. He is wearing it until Huia's hand is grown enough.

"Therefore," argues Humpty, who in appearance out-humpties Humpty Dumpty, "two years at the very least have propagated by, but more likely three. There was a miscarriage up the lane which could make it four. What price the survival of the human race? But, like, we've all got to do our bit at home to replace the manpower in France." He leans across the historied counter and whispers, "No one can accuse me of not doin' my bit since yours truly came back from the front; there are any number of little Humptys, brown and white, runnin' round This Side, comin' up nicely to supply the next war." He leans back and roars with laughter.

We're not beyond picking the seasons though as they follow one another; anyone can see it is autumn at the moment by the leaves of the willows turning and by the gold of the poplars marking the resting places of those who have departed . . . gold trees reflected upside down in the slowly moving water.

Toward evening—we know it is evening—a canoe puts off from the bank of That Side and sets off over the river. In it are Huia and Memory and Sire paddling back from That Side to This, all chanting a paddle song the old one has recently taught them, keeping instinctive time with the paddles, which is one sure time they know—any instinctive rhythm. It is in Maori of course.

> Behold my paddle!
> See how it flies and flashes;
> It quivers like a bird's wing
> This paddle of mine. . . .

But as they reach This Side landing an unrest stirs in Huia. Her allegiance to her koro on That Side confronts her feeling for Puppa on This Side. In the crossing of the polished surface of the river is the crossing from the brown to the white, although she's too young to know it, and the emotional racial transition is not polished like the face of the river holding the gray of the sky in her waters and the glamorous gold of the trees; it is something with smudges on it, something with jagged angles. The racial transition is a sunken branch cutting the mirror surface. Not that she knows these things; all she knows at these times is that she doesn't like anyone else, while all that "anyone else" knows is that Huia is getting naughty: This Huia-kid she cheeky, ay?

As they get out, wade ashore and fasten the canoe, her mind is full of Puppa and the touching image of him. Is he all right? she wonders. She leaves the others without saying a thing and wet-haired and wet-footed scrambles through the coarse river grass up the bank in a short cut to the road and trots uphill through the roadside flowers till she comes to the bridge at the corner, where she pauses to collect her breath. She looks down upon the stream below, her thick hair falling forward over her face, all but covering her eyes.

To look at she's the merest sketch of a child, as insubstantial as the rain wraiths. With no offense whatever she could stand in for the Dawn Maid upon the eastern horizon. Yet let anyone take her on in a fight or let them try to catch her and they'll learn she is far from frail; she has the indestructibility of a forest vine that only an ax can sever.

Then off again along the up-river lane in and out of the trees like a forest creature skirting the bank of the river, jumping over roots, leaping over rills and up the rise to the clearing where she pulls up again.

But all seems well: she can hear Flower and Sue on

their new duet and can see the little boys playing. Not carrying in the wood as they're supposed to be doing, but making a house with it, from which she reads that Mumma is down the bank dragging up wood from the river. No large arrogant horse is tied to a stump indicating a visit from Mr. Dunn. Puppa is all right, she thinks. He is usually all right if Flower is there. At a more relaxed pace she trots down the path through the seeding foxgloves humming the paddle song.

As she draws near the house, however, she hears shouting, and the boys do too. They look up and hasten inside. Also the piano stops. Huia runs in through the porch to the kitchen and here is Mrs. Considine punching Puppa as he crutches desperately, crutches in jerks across the room trying to escape and shouting to God for mercy. Huia begins whimpering immediately, "Don't hit Puppa, Flower's mother," and the others try to get between them. But just as the river counts no cost when marching down the gorges, mudshot in flood, hurling logs, creatures and bodies upon her, so the flood in Mumma counts no cost, knows nothing of what she is doing. The next thing she has snatched a piece of wood and is battering at his face. There's a patch of shiny blood.

"Look out for the hole in the floor, Puppa." A child's voice, Simon's, self-appointed master of ceremonies.

Mumma retreats, recedes like the flood, and furiously puts the wood in the fire while the children shepherd Puppa to his bed in the corner. "After all I've done for him," Mumma puffs. "Wearing my fingers to the bone, bringing up his family singlehanded, standing on my two feet all day teaching school, dragging branches up the riverbank, doing the washing, keeping the big ones at school in town and the boys at their violin lessons. After all I've done for him, yet he gives no sign he loves me." She straightens and swings on the boys, "You bring in that wood, y'little fiends. It's that ladylove of his in London." They do bring in the wood, loads.

"When I can walk," from the corner, "I'll walk right out of this house and you'll never see me again. Pass me a towel, God damn it, someone."

"That's what he always says. That's all he goes away for. Then he waits for us to find him." But she is definitely cooling down. Flower finds a cloth and tends his face and Sue returns to the keyboard while the boys bring the wood in hundredweights. The two babies, Richmond and Clarendon, toddle their way to his bed and hold onto his knees. Then Mumma makes the tea and pours two cups and hands one to Susanna. "Take him his tea," she says, "and tell him to stop his shouting. It gets on my poor nerves."

"If only we had harmony in the house," Puppa from the bed in the corner.

Flower moves center stage and takes up Mumma's

66

voice, "It gets on my poor nerves." Then takes up Puppa's perfectly, "If only we had harmony in the house," and away goes everyone's laughter, which so pleases Flower that she goes on and on and the laughing bursts on and on until Mumma can hardly go and milk the cow nor Puppa drink the tea.

How glorious the very next morning. True there is no rain, but ah, the sun touch, the flower eyes, the tree shine, the bird talk, the scent of the thousand-jacket and, like deeply flowing tears, the flowing of the river. Indeed it is not unlike one of those mornings in Puppa's stories when one day when he woke up what should he find he could do but walk. . . .

But instead of finding he can walk he finds himself taken by sledge to the landing and by boat to Whanganui hospital where they learn later he has lost an eye. And the waiting family in the clearing reads later in a letter that when Daniel and Hamish visit him there . . . when he looks up and sees them walk into the ward, he puts down his book and cries like anything.

But in time he returns, not without pride in his smart new eyeshade. It doesn't get lost like his crutches or keep tripping everyone up all the time. As for the baby she thinks it is lovely and is forever reaching to get it.

Po, the night, has long since defeated Ao, the light, in their regular evening wrestle, the puriri tree at the window is more imagined than seen, the forest and the foxgloves are invisible altogether and the sky-father wears no stars. Indeed there could be no clearing at all but for the stealthy rain.

Puppa sits on his chair at the window with his hands upon his knees, one folded upon the other, and the children cluster round him in their white nightclothes. They could do with the window closed, since the breath of the river reaches in and quite a little rain, but it's not worth the trouble. Mumma would at once gasp for fresh air and the thing would be open again. Yet there must be something in all this open doors and windows winter and summer since no one is ever ill. There's never a cold among the children—that's left for other people.

He adjusts his eyeshade, clears his throat and changes the order of his hands, at which the chattering stops like magic. "Once upon a time there was a Maori boy called Mokohiti who lived in the pa at Hawaiki thousands of years ago. Now this boy . . ."

"Not a Maori story, Puppa," from the white ones.

"Now I once knew of a king of Spain who . . ."

"No, not a pakeha story, please, Puppa," from the brown one.

"Did I ever tell you the story of the man who bought a horse?"

"No."

"Shall I tell it?"

"Yes."

He clears his throat and sings:

> I bought a horse.
> I bought a horse.
> I sold it for a do-onk-ee-ee-ee-ee . . .
> Jerusalem!
> The donkey died.

"Is that all? "

"Yes."

"What, have you finished the story for tonight?"

"Yes. You didn't want the others I began."

Uproar for a moment until he begins again, with no criticism this time.

"There was once a little boy who had no father and mother. He was an ugly child; his face was covered with freckles, his hair was straggly, his clothes were torn and he had bare feet."

"You said it was good to have bare feet."

"So I did. However, everyone needs shoes of a kind on a very stony road."

"And you said my freckles were pretty," from Flower.

"Ah, so I did. No, now that I come to think of it, he didn't have freckles. He was ugly for another reason: he never did any thinking. He . . ."

"D'you have to think to be pretty?"

"You do to be beautiful. There's a distinction there. Well . . . one day as he was walking along a stony road crying his eyes out he came to a forest and there at the edge of the trees—what do you think he saw?" He pauses, hoping for a clue, since he doesn't know himself.

"A taniwha?"

"No."

"A witch?"

"No."

"A tohunga?"

"No."

"What then?"

"He saw a very very ugly dwarf, considerably uglier than himself."

"What was he like?"

"Since you ask—he had crooked legs, crooked arms, crooked feet, a crooked body and he used a pair of crutches."

"Did he have black curly hair, blue eyes and a fair flowing mustache?"

"Possibly."

"Did he have one eye or two?"

"He had only one."

"Then he could not have been ugly; he was like you and you are beautiful."

Puppa changes his hands again and looks out at the night.

"Go on, Puppa. What was his name?"

"Truth."

"But you have always told us that truth was lovely."

"Ah, that is so. Nevertheless, truth has this strange quality of appearing to be ugly on first sight. Now this little girl . . ."

"Boy."

"Boy. Thank you."

"What was his name?"

He thinks hard a moment. "Utility."

"How frightful."

" 'Where are you going, child?' asked the dwarf.

" 'I'm going in search of a mother since I have none.'

" 'Haven't you got a father who will do?'

" 'No.'

" 'Then why not look for a father instead?'

" 'I'm not so keen on a father. It's a mother I'm after, see? And I know just what she looks like. Her hair is as gold as a cloud at sunset, her eyes are as blue as a roadside daisy, her voice is like the sound of a stream at midnight and the fall of her tears is the blessing of God. There must be a spare one somewhere.'

" 'Oh, no doubt there is. I wouldn't mind coming with you.'

" 'I would like company,' replied the boy, 'but you are so awful to look at that when I find my new mother she'll run away from me.'

" 'Think so?' replied the dwarf. 'If she refused to have you just because your companion was ugly, then she wouldn't be much of a mother and you'd be better off without her.'

" 'Is that what you think?' asked Utility.

" 'That's what I think,' he replied. 'Which is the big thing about me: I think. And everybody knows that thought breeds beauty. In fact, Utility, when we have traveled a bit together and you have come to know me better you'll find me not so ugly.'

"The two, Truth and Utility, traveled together for years, not agreeing very well at first but in time growing to understand each other more. And the strange thing was that Truth had the capacity to change his form; sometimes he was a child, sometimes a bird and on occasion a small animal—until the morning came when, waking in a clearing full of foxgloves, Utility was astounded to find beside him a woman with golden hair. Looking closer he saw that her eyes were blue, as blue as a roadside daisy. 'It is you,' cried the boy, 'I have found you.'

" 'It is you,' she said, 'I have found you,' in the voice of a midnight stream.

" 'You are so beautiful,' said Utility.

" 'So are you now,' she said. 'You are so pleasant to look at that I'll change your name at once. From now on your name is Freedom.'

" 'Why do you call me that?' he asked.

" 'Freedom and Truth make excellent comrades.'

" 'Why didn't you come before?' he asked.

"Her tears fell upon his head. 'I couldn't find you,' she said.

"By the side of a murmuring stream
An elegant gentleman sat.
On the top of his head was his wig,
On the top of his wig was his hat.
On the top of his wig was his hat, hat, hat . . ."

"Are Freedom and Truth with us all the time, Puppa, and we don't need to search at all?"

"On the top of his wig was his *hat*."

A year or two beat by during which time Flower goes off to high school in the big outside world, taken by Rose, who keeps her. May made a bid for her too, and Daniel who is married with a home, and even Hamish wanted Flower. He has no money, being mid-university, but wants to share his poverty with her. Susanna, however, who is far from being the flower o' the flock, has to make her way daily to Raetihi on a bony cream horse. On these long lonely daily treks, though, she makes the best of it: she says poetry to herself or makes it up or tells herself excellent stories with herself as the permanent heroine. But she gets home to the clearing at night too late, too tired or too wringing wet to get her homework done and often in a dreadful temper. "What's this?" She snatches a jug on the table where Mumma has laid her a meal. "Milk, water or beer?" Crash . . . Mumma boxes her ears.

"The *world* will take it out of you," from Mumma. In fact, the world did.

It is a year or so—I can't say how many—of heart attacks, rent attacks, tank attacks and Dunn attacks, as Puppa likes to term it. Up comes the large frightening well-fed horse along the up-river lane, its tail swishing the bridal manuka to send the white blossoms cascading in pain, and the next thing he's at the door.

He's a man with deep eyes beneath ponderous black brows in true landlord style, and his graying hair, springing stiffly, grows too low upon them, all but eliminating his forehead. This low-forward-growing

74

hair gives his face a criminal look in keeping with his calling, according to Puppa, and never fails to frighten the children.

"Mumma, he's at the door," from the children diving under tables and beds. Not "Puppa, he's at the door"; in the final count it is she who is the protector as well as the breadwinner.

Mumma picks up the role of the classic schoolmarm, her lips severely together, and she moves to the door with dignity. "Yes, Mr. Dunn?"

"I want me money."

"What money?" Innocence.

"The money y' owe me."

"Go and pass Standard Three* before you speak to me."

Slam goes the door in his face.

And the next thing heard from under the beds is the tank splashing from its stand, the summer supply of water in the dust. After a cautious moment out come all the heads from beneath tables and beds to survey the new situation. Puppa has sat the whole thing out on his chair at the window. There comes a very hollow blank. Where is Flower to re-enact the thing and send it up in laughter?

It is Huia who takes mid-stage. "Yes, Mr. Dunn?" in Mumma's voice. "I want me money," in Mr. Dunn's voice. "What money?" all innocence. "The

* Standard Three: Fifth Grade

75

money y' owe me," sepulchrally. Now with severity, "Go and pass Standard Three before you speak to me." She slams the nearby door. Crash follows the laughter; Puppa goes into hysterics of falsetto notes, Mumma collapses on a chair in staccato shrieks while the children roll on the floor, the whole explosion positively electrifying the tui in the tree, who is unable to take off to safety.

When it is over Mumma pulls up with a brief sniff and brushes back her hair with a forearm. "Oh well . . . there y'are, y'see. That's y'curses for you." She wipes the palms of her hands on her hips as though ridding herself of something distasteful. "Now we'll have t'carry water from the creek."

"By the look of the rain," from Puppa, "the stream will carry itself here." And away goes the laughter again. Even baby Clarendon, who cannot understand, picks up all this laughter.

From Lance, "Couldn't we get Daniel to come home and fight him?"

"How could a wounded hero from the war lower himself to fight a servant?" from Mumma.

Sue, "Why don't you get the police?"

Lance, "Because Paul Dunn told me his father told him that if we did he'd put a match to the house."

Puppa, "Anything Harry Dunn could do to this hovel could not other than improve it."

"Hurray, hurray," from Simon, "now we've got no

76

water. We'll have to bathe in the rain with no clothes on and have a swim every day."

It is during this same summer, when This Side House is full of guests with white shoes and flowered dresses that gleam in the shade beneath the lindens over the road from the house, that Mr. Dunn comes again. What he can't stand is the way some guests have of sneaking over the corner bridge, along the up-river lane to lean on Puppa's sill. Too much of an humiliation. What enrages him most is that it is usually, no, always and without fail, the more important of them whose names he has seen in the passenger lists of the liners from overseas who make this pilgrimage. This time he chooses a time when they are all at school except the two last babies. No doubt there are ways, subtle ways, of handling the man, as Hamish tries to tell them, but Puppa doesn't know them or doesn't want to. When Puppa calls him "Mr. Utility," the children running home ahead of Mumma, having seen the hoof marks on the lane, actually see Mr. Dunn reach in the window and punch Puppa's head. They skim like birds back to Mumma, "He's hitting Puppa, Mumma."

As luck would have it Mr. Dunn and Mumma meet at the wood heap where she tosses down her parcels, seizes a piece of wood and cracks him over the face.

He snatches it from her, Lance passes her another and crack she goes again. He snatches the second one, she is passed another and on goes the bloody story till he staggers and holds his face. Blood is everywhere. "Look, kids, she hit me here. Look, kids, she hit me here," and gropes to reach his horse which Sue has long since untied, cracked on the rump with the trusty wood so that it bucked and vanished from the fray.

"That'll teach you a lesson," puffs Mumma. "Think you can intrude on the premises of a respectable woman, a trained teacher, and strike Mr. Considine? You ignorant skunk. Why don't you read a book and improve yourself?"

In the evening when tea, heart attack and dishes are over, Huia turns from the piano and taking up the Dunn voice and holding her face moans, "Look, kids, she hit me here. Look, kids, she hit me here." Then in Mumma's tones, "That'll teach you a lesson. Think you can intrude on a trained teacher? You great big ignorant *skunk*. Why don't you read a book and improve yourself?" At which the household recovers in no time.

Mumma dries her eyes with the back of a hand. "But what did you *say*, Richie, to make him start?"

"All I said," from the bed in the corner, "was something utterly inoffensive. A mere morsel of philosophy. I said, 'It would have been better, sir, had you pursued virtue in your youth before the worldly demands of utility clouded your mind.' Is that anything to punch a man for?"

No one minds overmuch however two seasons later in the winter when he does, as he has threatened to do, come up when they're all at school and take the windows out. Mumma is passionate about her fresh air. "See?" in victory. "I'm always opening windows after you. Perhaps this will teach you." She makes the tea with some satisfaction and sends one per child to Puppa. "Come on, Huia. Make us laugh."

During this period of a year or so, the children toiling back from the forest with their load of funguses one Saturday—"We'll soon have enough to sell and to buy Puppa a lovely wheelchair"—come upon the astonishing sight of Daniel himself, so big, sitting on the black box at the foot of Puppa's bed crying, a big man crying, can you believe it? Not bawling as Trelawny does in the middle of the night waking everyone up because he is poor, or moaning as Huia does toward dawn—soundlessly, passionlessly, waking no one up but like nothing they have seen before. And as they gravitate into audience formation, instinctively and respectfully, they learn that he has not returned from the big outside world to thrash the Dunn, nor because of his war wounds, but simply to cry to Puppa, like Richmond when somebody teases him or like the baby when she's hungry. It turns out he is crying for nothing less than his first wife, Kaa Brice Clarendon,

Huia's mother, who so selfishly spends her time in the ground beneath a poplar. "She calls me, Puppa," he says. "I hear her calling me."

After all that time and Huia nine, no, eight I think. Through the war and everything, not to mention being thoroughly married and all that to a pakeha wife. A great big broad young man who could simply kill hundreds of Dunns with one hand tied behind and blindfold. Crying to Puppa—fancy! Just as the children do when they've got some chilblains or have cut a foot or something or when one has been teasing another, "I'll tell Puppa on you—oo," they wail. And now here is Lieutenant Considine of the British Navy telling Puppa on someone. And whom is he telling on? He's telling on Huia's mother. Why, what did she do? She *died.*

"I think I'll follow her, Puppa, soon."

"It's only," from Mumma, "your war wounds, Danny, and they'll get better."

"Puppa, if my wounds take me I want to be buried with her."

Not that he is pleased with Huia, his and Kaa's daughter, as the days go by, not after hearing—and *seeing*—how naughty she's been. Nor does she seek his approval, but when she finds her father here she lurks beneath the tree outside the window, one foot twining round the other, and furtively biting a nail. And when her father speaks to her and tells her to be a good girl and a credit to her mother she hangs her black head in a manner not witnessed before.

"If you don't behave yourself," gently enough from Daniel, "I'll send you back to the pa. It strikes me, young lady, that you've got more of your great-grandfather's melancholy in you than is good for you. You seem to have more Maori in you than appears in your face. Now pull yourself together, my lady, and behave yourself. If I come this way again and find you misbehaving I'll take down your pants and smack your bottom and send you back to the pa."

"It's that Togi," from Mumma, "who spoils her. He simply ruins her. He makes an absolute fool of himself the way he dotes on her. When she was a baby he wore her round his neck like a scarf. And *sulk?* My goodness, you should see her sulk. There have been times when I was as like as not to break every bone in her body. She certainly richly deserved it. But I've never laid a hand on her."

"Only because you couldn't catch her," from Lance.

Mumma sniffs briefly in admiration. "I must say she can run like a hare."

"And Danny," from Sue, "she drinks the cream from the top of the milk when no one else is looking and she stole some lollies from the store. And she plays with the Maori boys all the time, Memory and Sire and them, and never with the girls." She swings from a branch in the tree.

Daniel steps out over the sill and beneath the tree and kneels to Huia's level, and looks up mildly to Sue in the tree above him. "You don't seem to like my daughter, Sue."

"She called me a white maggot once, that's why."

"Oh?"

"And Danny, and Danny . . ." from Trelawny in another branch, "you know what else she did? She lit a fire in the school playground and it went through the fence and it took the whole village to put it out . . . she did."

"Don't send me back to the pa, Daniel."

"Say 'Father.' "

Rainstorm of tears, "No."

Gently enough, "I will send you back to the pa, you know, if you don't be a good girl like your mother."

"I don't know what she was like. She stays dead all the time. She's always under the poplar."

"She was always a very good girl."

"Don't send me away from Puppa."

Mumma from inside the window, "Let the child stay. She's all right, Danny. They're making her out to be a monster. But she's not. She doesn't hit the little ones as some of them do. Besides—" with pride— "we're never likely to hear such piano again . . .

82

marvelous. That's one thing she never has to be told twice—practice. Don't you think so, Richie?" She smiles her little smile. "And she makes us laugh, Danny, y'know. Just like Flower. What more can you ask from a child than that?"

Daniel straightens to Mumma's level at the window, his head knocking a branch. "I'm glad you speak like that, Mumma. As a matter of fact, her mother wanted her to be brought up European. They were Kaa's last words to me." A tear reappears. "And the old boy on That Side wants it. He respects the European culture."

"I want to stay with Puppa," weeps Huia, possessed. Simon joins in, then Puppa, then the two babies catch it, believing it to be the thing to do. But Trelawny and Sue remain dry-eyed and no one has seen Lance weep yet. "I'll be a good girl, Daniel."

"All right, all right." He picks her up. "You can stay with Puppa. Now you stop crying and I'll tell you something. You know your mother's greenstone she wore all the time—that your koro wears under his clothes to keep it warm—well, you're to wear it soon. You're to keep it always warm. Your koro said that when you're good enough you're to wear your mother's greenstone."

"I'll be a good girl, Da . . . Father."

. .

When this latest valley shower is over and Daniel has gone, and when Huia is found to be missing, everyone knows where she is. She is where she always is when she's upset for some reason—brooding in the forgotten meeting house in the shadows of the forest. Just like the dark-haired princess in one of Puppa's stories. Moreover, her ancestor Tikawe is there carved on one of the panels and even the tree god, Tane Mahuta, god of the forest and birds. You can spend till dark there cleaning the cobwebs from the occult carvings and polishing their paua eyes; she's at one with the other forest creatures there, furred, feathered or haired.

Time staggers by . . . laden. You'd wonder how time could carry the load of exploding life in This Side—in This Side alone. Time looks like Mumma sometimes after school, dragging her two feet through the dust on the lane, weighed down with parcels of food and a trail of children drawn out behind. Mud on her turned-out toes in winter and a fringe of it on her skirt.

ACROSS the road facing This Side House stands a row of lindens. It is quite dry beneath the wide branches like a wide long room. Here you can pick up the talk of the village and of the guests too as they lean on the trunks, gather in groups, sit on the long timber seat there or gaze down upon the river. And you see the kind of clothes they wear out in the big far world, the flowered or striped dresses of the ladies, the white shoes and socks of the children.

Pakehas pass through in their preoccupied way, booted and coated against the rain; Maoris appear and disappear in face-wet disarray, not covered from the rain at all, barefoot, brown-eyed, black-haired and serene; guests with their glistening umbrellas pick their shod way through the rain pools and the stones to talk a while here of the war or deplore the disappointing condition of the river they have paid so much to see. Meeting, movement . . . intimacy.

After school in the afternoon the children wandering down the road from the school on the hill often pause and play here. Drifting in from the rain with the others Huia is soon playing hopscotch with Sire and them, Mai's adopted ones, but soon they are learning Togi's new song, swaying gently at the hips, gesticulating and tapping a rhythmic toe, until she sees the other Considines moving off and joins them. They leave the shelter of the trees, run down to the store and hang about the veranda watching the coming and going, peering through the door at Humpty, plump, pin-eyed and pink behind the wide counter, joking with the men from the mills or sharpening his wits on the idle guests to roar with laughter at his own jokes. Even in winter they loiter here, Maoris and Europeans alike, except the Dunn children, Paul and Eva, who go straight into This Side House.

Lurking on the veranda this winter afternoon the children watch Mumma buying her groceries . . . Huia idly twirling a poi. They watch parcel by parcel being wrapped up and pushed over the counter to her by the irrepressible Humpty until there's quite a pile before her. There'll be some sweet new bread in those parcels and maybe some luscious sausages to eat with the browned potatoes. "Come and help me with the parcels, please," she calls.

Then they see the Dunn appear and walk behind the counter. The whole interchange following is simple and short as tragedy often is. "Got any money?" he asks.

"Not today," rather timidly, "but I'll pay at the end of the month."

Nothing more is said but his long arm reaches slowly across the counter, encircles the parcels and draws them all back to him, and Mumma comes out not speaking. And that's all there is to it.

They trail behind her to the corner but Huia follows no further; she takes the down-river road to the landing where she unties a swaying canoe on the muddy water, higher up the bank than usual. But the surface of the water is smooth enough, and if you paddle upstream against the current you'll end up in the right place on That Side.

Reaching the meeting house later she sits cross-legged among the others before the very old one beneath the carven image of Tane Mahuta, god of the forest and the birds. All the trees are Tane's children and most people say what a shame to see them falling beneath the saw of the pakeha, beyond the rim of the valley. Indeed the Maoris say that the great forest god will certainly revenge himself on the slayers of his children, remembering that he has already done so in the past in the form of a thundering flood rising forty feet up the bank; but that next time, to make his point clear, he will see that the flood is fifty feet up the bank. They say that the Tohunga Makutu at this very moment is composing special revenge chants for the occasion.

Huia takes a cautious look at the carving of Tane; in the glare of his iridescent eyes and in the tension of his lines there is the same expression he wore at the moment of his greatest effort in lifting the sky-father on high . . . a fifty-foot flood would be nothing to him. But the old one is beginning the lesson and she turns back to him. His face is not unlike Tane Mahuta's with its wrinkles and tattoo and fierceness.

"O young ones," he begins in Maori, looking beyond them, "attend.

"In this way the beginning,
In this way the creation.

Desired Tane Mahuta a wife.
Formed he a woman-shape from the earth,
Lay he his body upon it,
Breathed he his life into it,
Rose the earth-formed shape, a maid.

Took the earth maid to wife Tane,
And was born from them,
From Tane Mahuta and his earth maid,
The first man;
The first being wholly mortal,
Tiki.

"Repeat you this chant after me . . ."
The young Maoris take to this chant quite well, since it carries a story in it; it is the recitation of their genealogies back through the centuries to the arrival of the canoes that bores them, miles and miles of complicated names. . . .

Toward evening, as night is peering over the rim of the valley eying his opponent day, Huia is recrossing the river, but Memory is with her this time. Memory is a slave-born Maori but overarticulate and boastful, making out he's afraid of nothing, least of all Maori tapus and curses, spells and such. Even the taniwha in the river he does not fear, or claims that he does not. Older Maoris nod their heads in warning, "This young man, Memory, he run into trouble some day. The tapu it stop that long tongue one day."

But he is a young man who knew Huia's mother well and he's often at hand when Huia comes over. Theoretically he's a servant of the Te Renga Renga, but since there's little serving to be done the old one allows him to work with Togi on the boats for the Dunn. Personally he's a devoted follower of Captain Togi, from whom he's had orders to keep an eye on Huia, which he does at the moment with the river full. He swings the one paddle as though it were one of his limbs. "You doesen' want to be on this big water, ay, Huia, all on your lonesome?"

Huia tucks her poi in her belt and doesn't answer but looks down into the water colored with the soil of the distant hills naked from the ax of the white man. The rain has stopped dripping from the rain mat above and the sun, withdrawn for the night, has left the gold of himself on the clouds to the west. She stares into the depths for the water monster, then forgets it and thinks of Puppa. Is he all right? She has stayed away too long.

Then she recalls the old one. Is he all right or is he lonely for her, the only one left of his family? She senses division and faint distress and at this age knows she does. It seems that her canoe is constantly on the dangerous surface of the river, pulled by both the Maori from That Side and the English from This Side. In her unrest she sees both the black-haired mother, under a poplar, her father was crying for, and the fair one recurring in Puppa's stories with hair as gold as that cloud up there. Puppa must have known a woman like that to be often describing her. To have a mother like that . . . in her one's canoe could make a landing.

Memory fastens the homemade craft and the two of them wade ashore, but still the discomfort, division and alarm at the interracial crossing. The tender adagio Puppa has taught her, running at the back of her mind, is confused with discord; it has taken unto itself a forceful Maori rhythm the composer never meant. Leaving Memory with barely a word she climbs up through the river grass instead of taking the road. "You all right, ay, Huia?" Memory calls after her. "Me, I go back over."

"Some day," other Maori children have told her who have got it from the adults, "you be rich, ay, Huia? When your koro he die then you get those rent. All by your lonesome you get those rent. Ay, Huia? Then you be rich." In her childish way as she runs along the lane up-river she considers this; if it is true she knows what she'll do . . . she'll buy her way

90

through this biracial conflict. She'll buy Puppa into a position where she'll no longer worry about him, then she can relax and be a Maori, a Maori and nothing else, on one side of the river only. She'll buy a great big house, a grand house for Puppa and the rest of the family away from the Dunn and the clearing, where he'll be warm all the time, have plenty of food and no one will want to punch him. But it might be lies and not true at all.

Running in from the twilight to the kitchen, she finds Puppa quite all right. Amazingly it is Mrs. Considine who is not. For the first time Huia recalls the scene in the store when the Dunn took back her parcels. Flower's mother is lying back in a chair with the rain upon her through the paneless window and crying for all to see. "I'm supposed to be the breadwinner," she whispers, "but where is the bread?"

The following morning is a Saturday when Mrs. Considine gets up early to do the washing before she milks the cow and gets the wood, but when the children wake and wander through the rooms inquiringly they are astonished to find she has not risen early. They find her still in the big double bed in her room with no less than Puppa beside her, in bed too. Neither does Puppa get up to make the tea and cook the porridge for them. Seemingly too happy for action both of them lie there just smiling at the children who from long practice supply the audience. The babies are crawling over the bed and even Trelawny's not bawling. For the first time in her life Huia lights the fire and for the first time in known memory Susanna makes the tea.

The strange thing is that many months later some more baby clothes for the Belgians appear on the sewing machine in the front room. Lucky little Beljuns. . . .

Kei muri i te awe Kapara
E tu ana he tangata ke,
Mana te ao, he ma.

—An ancient oracular utterance

Which means:

Shadowed behind the tattooed face
A stranger stands.
He is white; he inherits the land.

THE evening is lovely.

True, it is not raining but still it is lovely. The puriri stands at the window motionless and shadowy, the forest mysterious and still, and between them the clearing, without the foxgloves which have died down in the winter. Water voices drift up from the river, the tui lets fall an occasional note, his signature to the evening, while from the forest emanates an odor made up of all the winter decomposition and all the summer blooming; exotic, pungent . . . heady.

It is the enchanted moment when day faces night, a magic time which holds in itself a capacity for improbability unlikely in the daytime. The fire is still going in the stove with one overlong arm of wood beckoning from the firebox, while moths and other night-winged creatures make a freeway of the window.

Mumma has finished her singing practice accompanying herself at the piano and reaching to any note the music calls for in her sure sharp soprano, and with a final cup of tea and a sigh has taken herself to bed. The children are grouped round Puppa's bed, some on it, some round it and one underneath it. Huia holds the new baby, Trelawny the old one, and there is cheerful quarreling among them.

Puppa moves, puts his crooked legs in an easier position and fumbles backward to adjust his pillows, but his stiff arms fail to manage and Flower is not here to do it for him. Susanna is too occupied planning a brilliant future, Lance can't think in terms of pillows, so Huia passes the baby to Simon and fixes the pillows just how he wants them, then sits and takes the baby again. This last baby, the eleventh or twelfth—I don't think it's the thirteenth—is called Déodonné which means "Gift of the gods." For your information it is a girl. It is Richmond who is under the bed.

Puppa leans back on his pillows, folds one hand upon the other and clears his throat for action. Like magic the quarreling stops but he doesn't begin as expected; he is looking over the heads of his audience through the window to the twilight and talks to himself as he does on occasion. " 'But when Night is on the hills, and the great voices Roll in from sea, By starlight and by candlelight and dreamlight She comes to me. . . .' "

"That's not a story."

No answer.

"Puppa?"

"Beg your pardon?"

"That's not a story, I said."

"Why, was I telling a story?"

"You know very well you were."

"God 'pon m'soul, so I was. Where did I get up to?"

"You haven't even started."

"Confound it, I thought I'd finished."

"You have not finished at all."

"I'll have to make a start then. Now . . . many years ago when I was a boy . . ."

"Oh we've heard all about when you were a boy."

He tries again, "One day when I can walk . . ."

"Oh, Puppa, we've heard that *millions* of times. Can't you tell us something new?"

"It's my turn," from Huia, "for a Maori story. I'm a Maori, don't forget."

"Now I once heard of a Maori boy who . . ."

"No, a princess," from the white ones, "with hair like a cloud at sunset."

"No, no," from Lance, "we've worked out that princess business. Get on with this story about this boy. I'll put up with him being a Maori."

". . . a little Maori boy called . . ."

"Not *little*," from Lance. "Make him my age."

". . . a Maori boy about Lance's age called . . ."

Pause.

"Rikirangi," from Huia.

"A Maori boy called Rikirangi who lived in the pa at Hawaiki. Now this Rikirangi happened to be another of these people who are blessed—I mean cursed —with curiosity, but this curiosity of his took an unlikely form: he had a passion about the sun. He wanted to find out exactly where the sun rose in the morning and how it rose and what for. He wanted to have a jolly good look at it and that's why he was so often seen in Hawaiki staring toward the east in the morning. So . . ."

Huia, "Puppa, I know about Hawaiki. My koro told me about Hawaiki. 'Hawaiki nui, Hawaiki roa, Hawaiki pamamao. Te honoiwairua.' "

Sue, "There she goes talking Maori again."

Lance, suspiciously, "What does that mean, anyway?"

"Hawaiki great, Hawaiki long, Hawaiki far away. The reunion place of spirits. See? Hawaiki is the faraway, far-ago home of my race, in the west where we came from in the first place and where we go when we die. I'll meet my mother there when I die, and my grandmother and all my ancestors." She holds the new baby with feeling.

The moment of magic in the clearing is over and darkness is frankly present but no one lights a candle.

". . . in the pa at Hawaiki. As I have said he wanted to find out how and where the sun rose for to him the sun was his great lord and responsible for his life. He wanted to meet him face to face and pay him every homage. If ever I were dying, he told himself, I know my lord would revive me.

"Yet beyond the pa was the ocean, in the ocean were many islands with hostile boys, and beyond them all, according to a seer, was an old white man who was known to covet greenstone and who had already killed many a colored boy to gain this greenstone.

"However, so great was Rikirangi's desire to greet his lord that one morning as the sun was rising he rose also and, leaving his greenstone behind him and taking only his mere and cloak, he passed through the pa gates, mounted his canoe, took up his paddle and set off upon the ocean eastward.

"Quite soon he arrived at an island and the moment he landed the boy there struck him. At once they were fighting. They fought long and hard, being fairly matched; sometimes it seemed that Rikirangi would win and sometimes it seemed the other. At length, however, after a cunning blow from Rikirangi, the other fell and failed to rise. Almost ready to fall himself, Rikirangi took a feather from the other's cloak and added it to his own but did not take his greenstone since it is a thing to be cursed to take someone's greenstone. Then he returned to his home in Hawaiki and washed the blood from himself.

"After a few days, feeling refreshed and rather pleased with his victory, his curiosity assailed him again. Sitting each morning watching the sun he decided to try once more. After all, he reasoned, I have defeated one boy and feel the stronger for it. Moreover I have a very fine feather added to my cloak that I've never seen in Hawaiki. Taking up his mere and wearing his cloak he again took the sea eastward.

"Soon he came upon a second island and a second fight took place, but this time Rikirangi won with a little less difficulty and as his opponent lay on the ground writhing from his wounds he took from the other's cloak a piece of weaving which he added to his own, but once more he left the greenstone. This time, however, he did not return to Hawaiki but settled on the island; he cleaned his wounds, admired his cloak and watched the sun rising.

"But not for long. After a time of rest and preparation he took to the sea once more, eastward, and conquered a third island. Again he failed to return to Hawaiki, being by now a long way from home. He settled in the home of the vanquished and watched the sun rising.

"Again he goes eastward; another conquest, another rest; another conquest, another rest, each time adding to the richness of his cloak and always leaving the greenstone, until he was far from his home in the west. Also by this time he had gained in strength, not to mention combat experience. I am ready, he thought, for any old white man, wherever he may be. Have I not proved myself a worthy descendant of my illustrious people? How proud they will be of me when I return, as I certainly will return to Hawaiki, far across the tide to the west. For some time Rikirangi sat in the morning turning over these things and marveling at the glory of the rising sun.

"Indeed, this particular country on which he had landed had everything a boy could want, from food and water to clothing and weapons, and he stayed here a long time. This land was better than Hawaiki and as for the greenstone he never took—this piece on the breast of the boy he had defeated was the loveliest he had seen. He changed his mind and took it, exchanging it for his own. As for his own cloak, by now its richness was worth a boy's life to preserve. In a glow of achievement he put a huia feather in his hair, deciding to stay forever in this place and to forget the rising sun. When the time came for him to die his spirit would return to Hawaiki.

"But one morning just as the sun was rising in more splendor than he had ever witnessed before, who should land on the island but a white man, the old white man the seer had spoken of, who, seeing the wonderful new greenstone, struck the boy at once. Rikirangi reeled and before he recovered was struck again and he fell. But as he lay smarting and panting he felt the sun, and, grasping his mere, he leaped to his feet and dealt the white man a blow.

"Long and bitter was the battle that followed, the youth, vitality and experience of the boy matching the decadent white man. Rikirangi put into practice all he had learned from his previous battles and swung his taiaha with telling effect but, although he was determined never to give up despite the advantage not being his, it became a losing fight. For the white man had a superior weapon which he had never seen before. At length Rikirangi was dealt a stunning blow that felled him once and for all, and the white man left him lying as though he believed him dead.

"But he snatched at once for the greenstone and without a second glance at the dying boy he sat down to examine it.

"Presently, however, Rikirangi regained consciousness and stirred. Opening his eyes he realized what had happened: his cloak was severely torn, into the fern was running away his life blood, there sat the white man fingering the greenstone while across his face poured the rising sun.

"I am dying, he thought. Now I shall never reach the rising sun. He closed his eyes to prepare his spirit to return to his home in Hawaiki, and as he lay dying he lived again for the last time those inspiring moments in Hawaiki at sunrise.

"But as he did so, again there stirred in him this

inspiration of his lord, the sun. Indeed, lying there in the fern with his life blood wasting, could he not still feel the warmth of his rays? Suddenly he decided not to prepare his spirit to return far across the tide to Hawaiki—not yet, anyway. The white man already had his greenstone so what more could there be to fear from him? He would rise again like the sun and continue his journey eastward.

"Padding his wounds with the ground fern he climbed shakily to his feet, wrapping the remnant of his cloak about him. For a moment he absorbed the glorious warmth into his chilled body, then took a few steps forward.

"At the sound of his steps approaching the white man looked up astonished. 'I thought I left you dead,' he exclaimed.

" 'I was dying,' replied Rikirangi, 'but I wanted so much to see how the sun rose that I decided not to die. No sun rises in the land of spirits.'

" 'You have risen by yourself,' cried the other. 'That is no less wonderful than the rising of the sun.'

" 'There is little other thought in my mind than of rising; rising again and again.'

" 'Indeed,' replied the white man, 'I have lost after all; I am defeated by my own admiration.'

"He began washing Rikirangi's wounds in a nearby stream, bound them with strips from his own clothing, and gave him water to drink. He restored the huia plume to his hair and tried to repair his cloak. 'A boy of your caliber,' he remarked, 'is certainly worth knowing. I have learned much from you. I shall be proud to protect you.'

" 'Will you,' asked Rikirangi, 'return my greenstone? It will bring a curse upon you.'

" 'I will not return your greenstone.'

"But the white man did nurse Rikirangi back to health and, side by side they lived together in the risen sun."

There is silence in the old dark room. Upon the sound of the river Puppa's voice still lies in the air. Suddenly in her passionate Maori way Huia bursts out crying. "I know," she weeps, "I know."

Sue, "Who was that white man?"

"Civilization," Puppa.

"I know that," Huia repeats.

"It sounds sort of true to me," from Lance. "Is it?"

"It's an allegory."

"What's an allegory?"

"It's one story told under the image of another."

"I'm no wiser."

"A big complex event told in a simple story."

"The story of what?" from Sue.

"The story of my race," weeps Huia. "How they left Hawaiki centuries ago and traveled eastward, island by island, until they got to New Zealand. Then

104

the white man came. My koro tells me all about that but only in hard chants. Not in a lovely story like this."

"Those were jolly good fights," from Lance. "What were they about?"

Puppa answers, "They were the battles with the new environments and peoples as they migrated eastward." He reflects a moment. "The big fight at the end with the white man—that was the Maori wars— when we took their land and impaired their culture." Another slow pause. "Yet the Maori recovered by himself. The Maori race is the only colored people to my knowledge which is rising again on its own from the impact of civilization."

Huia with emotion, "When I grow up I'll see that my race rises again and I'll see that it stays risen."

"By the side of a murmuring stream . . ."

"Don't sing that yet, Puppa," Huia pleads through extravagant tears. "Was it a kiwi or korowai cloak that Rikirangi was wearing? Both are ceremonial." The baby girl, Déodonné, in her arms awakes. "Did you mean the Maori culture by the cloak? The white man tore it, then helped him to mend it. My koro tells me all that."

"An elegant gentleman sat . . ."

From Sue, "Were the Maoris first in New Zealand? Then the white people came after?"

"On the top of his head was his wig . . ."

105

"I can't see," from Lance, "why Rikirangi wanted to see the sun rise all the time. You can see the sun wherever you are."

"That was the Maori ambition. He doesn't seem to have it now."

"Yes he does, Puppa," from Huia. "I've got Maori ambition."

"On the top of his wig was his hat . . ."

"But it's a jolly decent sort of story," from Lance, "even though it's about Maoris."

"It's a lovely, *lovely* story," from Sue. "Even though it's true."

"On the top of his wig was his hat, hat, ha—a—a . . ." he draws out this top note inordinately, continuing to hold it above their talking.

Richmond wakes beneath the bed and Trelawny, holding the old baby, accuses, "The white man didn't give Rikirangi back his greenstone."

". . . a—a—a . . ."

Huia, "That was the land."

". . . a—a—at. On the top of his wig was his *hat*."

ANOTHER winter is over with its river mists, floods, and rain wraiths; its flowerlessness, chilblains and guestlessness. Lance went away to school mid-year, since he was too restless in This Side to be taught; he questioned, contested, criticized and contradicted whether he secretly agreed or not. Daniel takes the boy into his home since he and Lance are both mad on wheels. He plans to apprentice him later in his own garage to take over should his wounds catch up with him. Mumma lets him go only on condition that he continue with violin lessons, but Puppa misses him. He has always been attracted to down-to-earth people the opposite of himself—his eternal beloved, Jenny, being one of these who never in the least understood him, nor he her, either. But that's how the world goes.

As for Sue, she still plods these eleven miles to Raetihi on the horse—"Bones" she affectionately calls him —since no one, even in response to Mumma's broad hints, has made an offer to take her. Although Daniel says he is prepared to pay her board in Raetihi if either Sue or the landlady can stand it, and there's some talk in his letters about buying her a small motorbike, but what price any motorbike on these apologies for roads? Only a horse can take it.

Since she has been at high school, however, Sue has found out a few things about herself. For one thing her hair, to date so mercilessly plaited, turns out to be quite wavy now it is released; and for another she finds to her astonishment that she is terribly clever

107

and can top most exams without even doing her home-work, being too late home. Also she's the official pian-ist at high school and in sport leaves the others stand-ing. All of which makes Mumma so proud that she takes on piano pupils after school on the school piano, including the two Dunn children, to see that Sue's books are paid for. And at the family table you hear her speak a poem to the children about, "But it's not for the sake of a ribbon'd coat, Nor the selfish hope of a season's fame; But the voice of a schoolboy rallies the ranks; 'Play up, play up and play the game,'" drop-ping a tear upon it. And Puppa indulges himself in a story to the children about an ugly duckling, except that this duckling is not a duckling but an amazing girl-ling, which Sue does not hear being too late home.

So that Huia is the eldest girl at home, since Sue might as well not be here. Trelawny and Simon are older than Huia but that means very little; there are three little ones below her: Richmond, Clarendon and Déodonné. She feels so necessary in the clearing these days and spends much less time sulking in the forgot-ten meeting house in the shadows of the forest.

Another winter is over and, with Déodonné off the breast, Mumma no longer has to ride the terrifying horse provided by the school committee for her to feed the baby at lunchtime. Puppa can feed her now whenever she chooses to come to him. The doors are shut tight when they leave for school now that the baby crawls; if the landlord took out the doors one day . . . but not even a Dunn would.

Once more my lord, the sun, fingers through the rain mat above to touch the tender hill breasts, urging their response to him, and they do with bright new growth. This early spring morning he is flicking the tips of the new-sprung foxgloves, no more than flannel leaves so far, when Huia staggers in the back door with an armful of wood. Mumma is milking Lily, the cow, and Puppa is stirring the porridge. Sue is too much of a dreamy academic to be of much use in the house, besides she has to catch her horse to be early on the road, so that Huia, forgetting the romance of her mother's greenstone and the greater romance of her rents to come, takes over in Flower's place. And she turns out to be quite practical and responsible and is an increasingly "good girl" since her father's visit. Maoris respect discipline.

"Is Trelawny doing his flute? Simon, set the table, there's a good boy. Richmond, take the music to Puppa and get that note right. Clarendon, you go to Puppa, there's a good wee girl, and get your hair combed. Sue . . ." tentatively, "you wouldn't wash baby's face, would you?" That's how Mumma addresses Sue, in a hushed sort of voice.

"Don't you know I've got to catch my horse? Get someone else to wash her."

Huia holds the wood in her arms. "Is the porridge ready, Puppa?"

His spoon circles the large iron pot gravely for the last time and he taps the spoon on the side. "The porridge is ready," with pride.

From the front room wafts the sweetest melody from Trelawny's flute, poignant and tearful, weaving in and out of the competing piano, and Huia pauses to listen. At length she turns to the hearth.

Puppa has begun on Clarendon's curls with the intentness of an artist. He flourishes the comb first, professionally, then with the cunning of a bird pinning down its prey the comb descends closer, closer till it alights on the small fair head. It alights with simple grace center back and moves down the parting. But just at this moment a piece of Huia's wood catches his foot to wrench it sideways. "God," and he drops the comb. Crash goes the rest of the wood on the hearth and Huia clasps the foot. "I'm terribly sorry, Puppa."

From Trelawny's flute comes the proceeding melody and Mumma is back with the bucket of milk. "Are y'hurt, Richie?"

"Oh my God."

Simon turns, "What are you doing to Puppa?"

"Is there no room for my wretched legs?"

"I didn't mean to, Puppa."

"Confound it, pick up that comb, will you?"

Once more he concentrates on Clarendon's hair, giving it his whole attention, Mumma begins straining the milk with all her abundant energy, Simon thinks it wiser to set the table, Trelawny and Richmond continue their practice, Sue actually does, for the first time in her life, wash the baby's face and hands, even her small fat feet, and Huia takes off outside. . . .

By the time the fingers of the early sun have felt further about the clearing the family sits down to breakfast; another long spring day is ahead of them.

Mumma's passions, like those of the river, are from a never-emptying source; touch them with a little rain on the hills, try banking them up somewhere, and down come the high muddy waters pulling everything down with them. On the other hand, give either of them a summer of innocent days and here is surprising beauty. One half-hour outside on an early spring morning with your head tucked in the flank of a phlegmatic cow, with the flow of the milk in the pail, is good for any soul.

No awful row blows up at the table, so that Huia whimpering under the tree stops under her own power and climbs in over the sill. Mumma speaks verse with tears in her eyes, "My beautiful, my beautiful, that standeth meekly by . . ." Beside the ungathered rice he lay . . ." and the permanent favorite, "They grew

111

in beauty side by side . . ." and Puppa says things like "When I can walk I'll make millions of money and we'll all live happily ever after."

So much can the sun in spring do when the fog gives him a chance. How profoundly a part of nature we are, how sensitive to her moods. The "harmony in the house" this morning is of the kind that could well produce diapers for the Beljuns.

But a few weeks later when the company in the clearing wakes to one of these fogs spewed up from the taniwha in the river, of the kind that doesn't lift till eleven in the morning, when the little ones are crying with chilblains and Mumma comes in frozen from milking Lily, unwittingly they all react. Between audible mouthfuls of porridge Mumma is not speaking verse but is teasing Puppa who shouts to God; inquiries are hurled to the ceiling as to the duration of his infirmity and there are references to his infernal and eternal subjection.

"Flower's mother," from Huia, "don't tease Puppa."

A short laugh is cut off by a mouthful of porridge, she lifts her plate from the table a little and lowers her face to meet it. "I told y'so," she nags. "I said y'sins would come back on you. And they have, they have, they have." The plate lifts higher and the face comes nearer. "And what's more it serves y'right."

"Bring me my crutches someone. Daniel, Hamish, Rose, God damn it. May, Flower, Susanna, God curse it. Lance, Trelawny, Simon, Huia. Richmond, Clarendon, Déodonné. *Anyone* at all. Bring your father his crutches. Let me get out of this hell." He hits the table with his funny hands in the old London style. A crash of plates and his knife goes spinning and skidding along the floor.

Huia climbs from her place on the form and approaches Mrs. Considine. "Flower's mother, don't tease Puppa."

The plate and the face of Flower's mother now almost meet but she lets through another brief laugh which ends in a final gollop. For a moment she examines the empty plate with inquiry and regret, then licks her lips, narrows her eyes and leans toward Puppa. "And what's y'shouting going to do for us? Does shouting help to bring up a family? Does it pay the bills and educate the children? Is it going to pay the nuns for the violin lessons and Trelawny's flute? Is it going to put shoes on feet? Is it going to put back the tank on the stand and replace pillaged windows? Will it chop the wood, milk the cow or drag up logs from the river? Tell me," voice thickening, palms upturned, "is it going to fill these mouths?"

Nearer and nearer to him, "What's y'shouting and raving done for us? D'you think I don't have enough? Inspectors shouting in the schoolroom at me, the chairman of the committee shouting at me, and that criminal scoundrel, Dunn? All shouting," up on her

113

feet, chair overturned, and pacing the length of the kitchen, "from daylight till dark. Orders from the minute I open my eyes till the minute I try to shut them. Even orders from that Maori over the river when I see fit to discipline his race. What about that, ay, what about that? D'you all think I'm no more than a servant paid t'do y'bidding?

"And now here y'are, here *you* are shouting orders too. *You* disciplining me. Who are *you* to discipline me? A fine English gentleman, but where's y'ancestral home now? Where are y'famous books? Where are the reviews and applause and payment and fans pouring in the door? Where has y'money *gone*? If it weren't for me none of you'd have a roof over y'heads. *None* of you would. Just my two hands and my two feet keeping the wolf from the door."

A pause for breath and she turns away as the level of the flood recedes. "If he loved me," to the stove, "it'd be another thing. There'd be a reason for my labors." Sinks in the chair again. "But what am I but a makeshift for all his fancy ladies."

"Flower's mother," touching her knee.

"Get out of my sight," the flood whips again. "Haven't I got enough t'do without feeding and clothing a Maori? Me bringing up a family singlehanded? Thirteen clever children? Where would their universities be, their nursing, their—their concert orchestras, th-their garages . . . all their successes in the outside

114

world and their magnificent independence were it not for me—the slave." The open hand beats the air in emphasis, "Yet here I am feeding a dirty Maori who will be as rich as Croesus. That's what y'expect me t'do."

"Stop, Flower's mother . . ."

"Don't 'Stop Flower's mother' me." A box on the ear sends her reeling to end up among the wood.

"Don't strike that child. O God, give me my legs. O God, release me from this hell. My crutches. Give me my crutches. Will *no* one bring me my crutches? Will *no* one obey me in this accursed house? Who am I? Only the father."

Trelawny unpetrifies himself, scrambles from the row on the form, runs and picks up the crutches on the floor beside him. Puppa fumbles with them, jerks to his feet and swings across the kitchen. "O God," he implores, "have mercy."

The river hurls one last boulder, the one that dammed it in the first place. Whispers, "I know where y'money's gone. It's gone on that wicked creature." She almost chokes. "*Jenny.*"

A sudden cry from Trelawny, "Look out for the hole in the floor, Puppa." But his crutch plunges through so that shouts of rage change to shouts of pain. Huia gets up from the hearth, the yellow dress that Togi has bought her at strange odds with the mud-shot scene, and crawls hand and knee toward him,

115

joining all the others in lifting him and dragging him to his chair by the window. He is white and trembling and the gay mustache that enthralled "that Jenny" in the days of his past affluence . . . it twitches as he whispers, "Have mercy on me."

With the hurling of the final boulder the flood waters are settling down into their routine channel and Mumma sniffs briefly. An arm brushes back her hair. "Well . . . there y'are, y'see. All your culture won't mend a hole in the floor." Then she steps forward suddenly in sanity. "Are y'hurt, Richie? You're not hurt, are you, Richie?"

He gazes through the window on the fog-dim tree standing there like a recording spirit and resumes his monologue with God, too soft to be wholly audible. "Is it that my spirit needs further discipline? What is your purpose, Lord, in continually plunging the steel into the furnace? Am I not fined, sharpened enough to be honored as your tool? What function have you planned for me? Have you in mind some universal idea for which to employ your servant? In which only the most tempered instrument will do? There are times, my Master, when the suffering, the torture, the white heat of agony all but pulverizes. The furnace may consume me like the frailest matchwood . . . into the dullest ash."

Mumma stands before him in a heavy way, a helpless sort of way; from her rather good head, broadening through her body downward to the wide hem of her skirt, a living elongated triangle, her hands hanging wide beside her, open. All the children group round them, the forgotten baby crying on the floor. In the blandest innocence she inquires of them, "What's been happening? Who's upset y'father?"

In time the company gets to the place where Mumma makes the tea, and as it runs from the spout of the teapot, steaming, light-catching and amber as a jewel, it glows reconciliation; in its wordless story it tells of the low watermark of the river reflecting the blue sky. "Here y'are," to Huia, "take him his tea." The river flows dreamily through its gorges reflecting the flowered trees.

But when Huia holds the cup before him Puppa doesn't see it. His one eye still stares out through the river fog loading the quiet clearing. Darkness persists in his single eye unrelated to his gay mustache and his cheerfully curling hair. Rigid, he sits, one sharp knee upon the other, elegantly posed and his hands locked upon them.

"Little darling, here is your tea," in the way of Flower.

No answer.

One slim arm encircles his shoulders. "Here is your tea, little darling."

"What did you say?" Turns.

"I said, here is your tea."

．．

It will soon be time to leave for school when Mumma gathers up the dishes for Puppa to wash when they have gone and Puppa is saying, "One day we'll all have finished being poor. When I can walk I'll make millions of money and dry every eye in the family. Day after day there'll be harmony in the house. I'll buy a lorryload of books and a boatload of oranges. The dolls I will buy will be the size of yourselves and each one will walk and talk. I'll buy you each an Arab steed and you'll all be dressed in velvet.

"And I'll buy your mother an enormous house, the grandest in the country, grander by far than This Side House, with wrought-iron gates, balustrades and romantic balconies. I'll provide an army of efficient servants bowing and scraping all day long and springing at her slightest wish." He glances at her gathering the dishes in the old enamel basin. "She'll never have to work again. You'll see her dressed in silk and satin and with buckles on her shoes. She can sing at her piano all day long and all night too should she wish it. There'll be no more chairmen, no more inspectors and no more Harry Dunns. Never again will she carry the smallest parcel, since tradesmen will deliver. When I can walk . . ." he adds.

"But if you don't walk, Puppa," from Huia, "she'll

still have all those things. When my koro dies and I get my rents I'll buy the lot myself."

"It sounds like a dream," from Mumma.

"It makes a good story," from Puppa. "It certainly tells well."

Softly and with no sound the fog heaves its great belly from the clearing and down come the hands of the sun to touch and to heal with his fingers. As Puppa wraps the lunches, ties their hair, tying Huia's off her face with string, he enlarges so ridiculously on the future that everyone laughs like anything. Indeed the company is so happy again by the time they leave for school that rages, like fogs, evaporate.

Little Clarendon, about two or three, goes to school with Mumma now, holding Mumma's hand, and only the baby stays with Puppa. Puppa stands with Déo-donné framed in the back door as in turn the others kiss them goodbye. The children lift their toes and skim down the path as though they had never known a tear. At the end of the path they turn and with a final wave to the tableau in the timbered doorway, of Puppa and Baby side by side, to be impressed on their memory forever, they race off down the up-river lane to catch up to Mumma and pass her. For this moment, at least, he is safe.

IN the valley of This Side there are many flowers, especially in the spring. The kowhai at the corner bridge is king of all the blooms, or thinks he is, and for a brief period of a few weeks he goes to some pains to prove it—to some pleasure to prove it, I should say. What he claims to the manuka, rata and thousand-jacket is that spring is not here until he is, boasting that the only color worth showing is gold. In which case he is in good company: so are the buttercups, so are some daisies and certain of the orchids gold.

But he's a squanderer at heart. He blows his whole wealth at one performance leaving nothing for the rest of the seasons, so that while the thousand-jacket and the manuka see out the summer he himself is finished. "An opportunist," from Humpty who sees him from the store, "but a damned good opportunist. Like, he gets in first, see? He grabs attention before anything else can do a thing about it. What do the guests remember when they have left This Side? It's yon kowhai over there. Why try to debate it? His bloom is the emblem of New Zealand."

Lovers like this bridge with the kowhai nearby, and not only the living but departed ones too. Here they cluster, whisper and haunt to re-enact their rapture. Whai Te Renga Renga loiters here to meet Brice again, to talk to each other about each other till they merge in their bodyless joy. Also whispers on this bridge dead Kaa Te Renga Renga, calling Daniel to his last appointment. And others who have departed.

So does Huia of the ngati Te Renga Renga come here, this young light walking proof of the existence of those before. In the easy way of a Maori she can sense their presence though she cannot define who they are. Without realizing it she thinks Maori thoughts when she pauses on the bridge, not necessarily of her immediate forebears but of her race in general.

There comes an afternoon in late spring when she gives in to her thoughts voluptuously and curls down beneath the showy gold of the kowhai here. After watching the tuis in it for a while guzzling up the nectar or fighting out their spring mating in the air, she takes out her homework book and her pencil and the next thing she is drawing the ceremonial cloak that occurred in a recent story: Rikirangi's cloak that was torn by the white man. So absorbed does she become that she doesn't hear the sound of another step that will repeat itself in the future when the stepper has done with living. Paul Dunn, the son of This Side House—he'll revisit this bridge one day, and re-enact this hour.

He's about twelve and ready for high school, and more like his mother than his father, in character that is; but he carries on the male Dunn line in the low-growing hair on his forehead and the too-heavy jaw. He leans over her shoulder, his hands pocketed. "You'll never wear a cloak like that. My dad says you're a mongrel."

It is some few moments before these words get through to this descendant of rangatiras and illustrious ancestors, but when they finally do her hand swings upward like Flower's mother's, the hand with the book in it. There's the resounding smack of book on flesh and the face, its mouth agape, reels back from her vision. "You white maggot," she hisses.

So high is the Maori running in her that there's no question of taking the up-river lane to see how Puppa is. With her face still hot from the racial insult, as hot as the one that was smacked, she takes the down-river road to the landing where she comes upon Mai unfastening a canoe.

Mai's houseful of adopted ones on the hill, together with a fluid company of friends, enemies, relations and lovers, is one of the sights of This Side, though she frightens the guests to nightmares. She is short and broad, her bulk unwieldy, there are dark spaces

122

between her teeth, there is hair on her face, she has several unnecessary chins, while her bulging black eyes—one is cast—heavy-lidded and wide-whited, have a leer that unnerves the taniwha. As for her hair —it is simpler to acknowledge it at once as stiff, black wire, a wig of spikes that could pierce the throat of a boar in the forest.

Yet Mai is a popular Maori. For one thing she knows her Maori medicines. She can lure an evil spirit from an ailing body as long as the body is a Maori's, and there is scarcely a chant composed in the last five hundred years with which she is not acquainted. And for another, she's a master of brewing. True, no one so far has caught up with her recipe for skull-splitter since she changes it arbitrarily, but a deep-worn track zigzagging up the hill to the copper in the back room is the tribute of the village to this brew. The sole known requirement of this recipe is that it must be drunk before it is ready—while still thick and green. That's the time to dip in a mug. For who *wants* to wait till it's ready?

Not that Mai has overlooked a husband—she remembered that—and even though they have never bred a child between them Tekaou is proud of his wife, understandably so. In and out of her dodging lovers the two remain seriously married.

It turns out that Mai is on her way to visit the totara tree on That Side in which Tane Mahuta, god of the forest, is said to abide on occasion—when he needs "to get away from it all." She's going to chant to him a prayer for another child and with fair hope of success, since any amount of spare children appear in the spring along with the valley flowers. Just because she walked on tapu ground in her youth so that her womb became barren, is that any reason in Maori thinking to forfeit immortality? What would her weaponed ancestors feel if she left no descendants? She could never show her face when she returned across the tide to Hawaiki.

The river is low today. The surface of the water is silky and green like the brew in Mai's big copper, but as the two of them cross each looks fearfully below for any sign of the taniwha. Not that he's likely to be there. Everybody knows he likes conditions for a decent drowning or two, his main dish being the souls of men whose bodies he belches back on the beach.

Mai proceeds to explain to Huia, who takes it all in gravely, how the level of the water depends on the tohunga who is responsible for the rainmaking chants.

> Is afraid, the tohunga, of the water monster.
> Wants, this monster, big water in the river?
> Sees to it the tohunga.
> Wants, this monster, little water?
> Sees to it the tohunga,
> This time, this time, this time.

Listens to him, the tohunga.
Respects him, the tohunga,
This year, this year, this year.

The one being, spirit or mortal
Up, down or across the river
Whom the tohunga obeys . . .
That is the taniwha,
The monster in the river.

Reaching the bank on That Side they fasten the canoe and part, Mai to her interview with Tane Mahuta:

Turns, O turn to me thy hidden face
O Forest God.
Chant I my prayer for another child
To Tane, the forest God . . .

and Huia to haka and poi practice. With an unusually strong sense of kinship she runs through the sun and the silt to the meeting house where Maoris young and old are lined up in vigorous song, gesticulating, swaying and tapping their feet in overwhelming rhythm. "Come on, young Huia," calls Memory, "you get in. You not a Maori for nothing, ay," at which there's a shower of laughter from the crowd. In the close hot air, possessed by the quickening beat of the tune, the melody and the harmony, at communal one with them all, it is true she's not a Maori for nothing.

By the time they disperse the rain has returned and the river is tinted with soil. Such is the weight of the rain . . . it can only have come from the tohunga's successful rainmaking chants. Where else could it have come from? The river has already risen a little by the time she returns with Mai, Whakaturia, Sire and them, with Memory on the paddle. No one chants the canoe song with the water in such a mood, with the taniwha undoubtedly below. Carefully they concentrate on reaching This Side since none wants his body to be belched back on the beach.

As the canoe makes its nervous way across the ponderously moving water, her inner world changes color and character. That Side is everything that is Maori, This Side in the clearing all that is English, each side demanding its inherited loyalty, while right here on the treacherous surface of the river is the recurring transition . . . this sundering feeling accompanying movement from one race to another. Where can her spirit fly like a bird to its nest where conflict is forgotten?

When she has parted from the others at the corner bridge she stands upon it and watches the turbulent water below, raindrops slipping from the tails of her hair and from the hem of her dress. Is Puppa all right? Flower would never have left him so long. That comes of being Flower and not an irresponsible Maori. But the muffled beat of Togi's boat pushing upstream with its mail and provisions restates how late it is. She sets off in the dusk.

Trotting up the lane she slows to a walk aware of the peopled silence, but the image of Puppa grows; in vital detail she sees his pale face, his hands, his withered body and his ever-present crutches. She sees him standing in the timbered doorway with the baby at his side as they looked back at him this morning. He is sitting by the stove stirring the porridge or stroking the browning potatoes, reading at the window or washing the dishes seated before the basin. He is laughing with the children in the morning, he is crutching desperately away; telling a story or cursing on a bank down the lane one evening. Now he gazes at the foxgloves with one blue eye, now he drinks his tea. Teaching them music, singing the tenor of the hymns Mumma plays on Sunday, poised on his crutches behind her. How could she have left him so long? Wretched unreliable Maori she is . . .

Day has overcome night by now and in the gloom the sounds assume shapes of their own: the water noises are talking bubbles, the shriek of the cuckoo a witch; the voice of the tui is a glistening woman and her own footsteps a following ancestor . . . maybe it is Whai, maybe Kaa, maybe Tikawe.

A Maori nervousness comes. The forest is a giant,

127

the river a taniwha and the manuka a ghostly bride. Even she herself is a haunting spirit who failed to depart to Hawaiki. She tries running for a while but slows to a walk again.

Suddenly there is a more violent image of Puppa, one she keeps carefully hidden: he is struggling down the back steps, there is someone beating him on the head with a piece of wood, he is shouting to God for mercy and trying to escape. . . .

She runs. She pushes through the noise ghosts, tree ghosts and water ghosts, through the pools and bridal manuka at the foot of the leaping place, splashes through the stream at Puppa's corner and jumps the risen roots until puffing, dripping and shaking she reaches the top of the lane where it narrows to the path, in her mind a picture of shiny blood, red on a white face. She stops and stares across the gloom at the square of candlelight, unable to move forward.

Suddenly in the silence the rain drops like a cloak upon a body. Heavily, comprehensive. It hisses on the grass, smacks at the leaves and cries out loud on the trees. Maybe she's too late. Brave with horror she tears down the path, the fern fronds flicking her legs, and bursts through the porch to the kitchen.

And what does she find but Puppa sitting at the stove stroking the browning potatoes, with Baby on his knee, his hair combed, mustache brushed—calm, elegant, English.

128

• •

During the night, however, the rain sets in with purpose. It sets in first on the naked hills beyond the western rim, on the defenseless hills where the soil is loose with no protective foliage—the ravished hills where floods are born to march down This Side valley. Then it includes the valley; the cloud mat that sits habitually dripping collapses altogether and down spills all its water on roof, on road, on tree. Down it roars on the home in the clearing so that Puppa puts down his book; in the candlelight he listens.

As the night deepens the thunder breaks and rain falls in greater body. He takes his pipe from his mouth and looks toward the window. The white of the lightning is the white of the furnace in which his Master tempers his soul. Susanna awakes and runs through the house hysterically blocking the windows, then Huia, stripped too suddenly of the garment of sleep, wakes taut, her senses bared. In the absence of sight, hearing is doubled. Unerringly the tumult stabs to the very heart of feeling . . . for an unmeasured moment a death of fear till realization follows: plainly the taniwha comes. He is outside, he is near. The taniwha is certainly on the roof and whom has he come to get? He's come to consume the spirit of Puppa so that he'll haunt the clearing forever. The din, the taniwha, the agony . . .

A sound begins in her throat, the close-lipped moan of a Maori. To her it comes from beyond herself as though Puppa were already mourned. She hears the quick thud of steps as Mrs. Considine takes over, the hysterics of Susanna. The taniwha has indeed come inside and her moans grow to shrieks: "Puppa . . . what's happened to Puppa?"

Ka kotia te taitapu ki Hawaiki.

—Maori proverb

Which means:

There is no recrossing of the tide to Hawaiki.

THIS Side dreams . . .

She dreams in her moment of summer as one dreams in the moment of love. She seems to have forgotten the winter behind as well as the one before. She flowers to her fullest as though summer were eternity holding the meaning of life. She opens and gives to her lord, the sun, as he fingertips her hills . . . refusing and qualifying nothing.

There is no rain at all. Week after week the sun makes love to the seductive valley beneath him, to the valley stretching her breasts to him. Mornings come still and virgin, noons ascend brilliantly to their heights of uncompromised emotion, curving over at the top into afternoons to faint in exquisite evenings. Flowers bask wide, birds toss notes like wasteful children; the forest parades are grand and royal round the encircling ranges, while lying at his feet like a woman in love . . . this slumbering siren river.

THE carved ancestors on the roro of That Side meeting house gaze across the river. The sun is in their paua-shell eyes, but on they gaze unblinking. It seems they are looking beyond the river and beyond the western ranges, indeed the focus of their iridescent gaze may not be geographical at all; they may well be gazing back over thousands of years into the distant past of their race, back across the tide to the west to the legendary home of the Maori: "Hawaiki nui, Hawaiki roa, Hawaiki pamamao. Te honoiwairua."

Beneath them on the roro Huia sits cross-legged before her koro, who is lying on bright-colored rugs. As usual there are several other old ones with him keeping him company, sitting about on flax-woven mats. There's nothing a Maori can do better than just simply *sit*, doing nothing, expecting nothing. In the kumara patch nearby, the next generation and the next are weeding the sloping rows while between them and the old ones play the children, grandchildren and great-grandchildren.

Huia squats beside him, his hand in hers, as he seems to be near his time. It has been suggested that he go to the hospital but it never amounts to more

134

than that. "I'll only be brought back in a box," he says. To Huia he appears to be already a spirit departed across the tide to Hawaiki, a spirit that has actually gone but forgot what to do with its body. At the moment his left-behind body would do credit to a panel on the wall among the other carvings.

She stares at his face in her wide, open childish way, unconscionably frank. She doesn't like it very much, it's too old. Personal love cannot bridge three generations; to Huia he is an old man who teaches her hard things and takes too long about it, while to him Huia is an important descendant, the most important of all, who must carry on the tribal culture, as well as his own blood.

At his great age his face is a puny one and might even have been ordinary but for its dual expression: the smile on one side and the scowl on the other give it a disconcertingly double look of both supplication and fire. Fierce is one eye, entreating the other—the fierceness of the spirit already departed against the entreaties of the human, the last message of a dying mortal.

Also his voice, once so resonant as to thunder the length of the river, has changed to something thin and eerie; the diction has retained its fastidiousness and its aristocratic cadence, but there is to it now a certain new impersonal quality as though he were reading something rather than speaking from himself. Lifted

135

to the theater pitch of a chant, it is impressively in harmony with the occult atmosphere of the ancient meeting house. Huia sincerely believes that the company of other old ones about extends beyond the visible; plainly the spirits of their illustrious ancestors occupy their carven counterparts, for the time being at least.

Nearly always there are other young Maoris with her but today there are not. They're pig-hunting in the forest, eeling in the river or making love somewhere. But in this climate of the already departed, as well as the surely departing, there's nothing hard in following the aged Te Renga Renga through the lesson he has for her—it is organically compatible.

"O Huia," he begins in Maori, "attend."

"Ana," from Huia.

"Say this after me: 'Has made the old paddle of Maori days . . .' "

" 'Has made the old paddle of Maori days . . .' " The others become quiet and listen.

" 'Many long voyages in its time . . .' "

She repeats it faithfully; Maoris excel in learning by rote.

"But has passed that time.
Are ended the old days of hands and feet,
The day of war.
Has dawned the day

When must walk in harmony with each other
Maori and pakcha;
Having the same aim in life.
Progress.

The day of brain, this.
Is sweeping on the tide of wisdom and development
And must go with it we.
Must be done the voyages of today,
With the new paddle of the pakeha.

When worn out is the old paddle
Is it not cast aside
And is taken aboard the new paddle?
Education is the new paddle of the Maori canoe.

Has dawned this day, O small Rangatira;
Is shaken
The foundation of the old Maori world.
The cradle of a new race
Is the remaining Maori land.

Knows this new race the stone
And yet the steel also.
Knows this new race the brown
And yet the white also.
Cannot return we.
There is no recrossing of the tide to Hawaiki."

The paua eyes of the ancestors confirm this, sepul-chrally, wistfully. And the brown eyes of the living do also, in soft sentimental tears. There is a silence that is pure Maori.

"You mean, O Koro, that we must live like the pakeha, we who are alive?"

"I mean that."

"Alive . . . we cannot recross the tide to Ha-waiki?"

"I mean that."

"Only when we die, then our spirits return to Ha-waiki?"

"That's what I mean."

"It must be nice to die then."

"I do not mean that, O Huia."

"But you'll be meeting my mother in Hawaiki, the reunion place of spirits."

"I will."

"And Whai and Tikawe?"

"And Whai and Tikawe and many others of your ancestors."

"Will you speak of me to my mother, O Koro?"

"What do you wish me to tell her?"

"Tell her that . . . tell her my hand is not big enough yet to wear her ring, the Clarendon ring. Togi's still wearing it for me. And she might as well know that—that . . . that I still don't wear her

138

greenstone. My father said I would when I was good enough. Tell her that I . . ." the tears appear . . . "that I try very hard to be a good girl but . . ." She does not finish.

He fumbles behind his neck to unfasten a gold chain, clumsily, and an old kuia does it for him. It carries a greenstone tiki which he holds close in the warmth of his hand.

"Am I going to wear it now?"

"When you have said the remainder of the survival chant, O mokopuna. Follow me now.

"Meanwhile
In thy blood runs the knowledge of the stone
Yet also runs the knowledge of the steel.
In thy blood the brown inheritance
Yet also the inheritance of the white.

Drink thou then the white culture into the brown
As the Te Renga Renga in generations gone by have
    drunk
The blood of the enemy,
The strength of the enemy.

Drink, O Maori, the strength of the white
For has dawned the day

When must walk hand in hand
The brown race and the white.

In this way only, O small mokopuna,
May the Maori continue
Toward the rising sun."

Again the paua eyes confirm, gleaming somberly.

"Can I wear the greenstone now, O Koro?" She twists about restlessly.

"This is the greenstone Takarangi. Your ancestors all wore it. Tikawe wore it, your grandmother Whai wore it, your mother Kaa wore it and soon you are to wear it. Your first daughter will wear it and her first daughter will wear it and so through the generations. It is passed over while the wearer is still alive so that it always remains warm. The greenstone Takarangi has never grown cold.

"This greenstone Takarangi is alive. It holds to itself the life warmth of generations of Te Renga Renga women. It was taken from the broken body of your ancestor Tikawe, after she had thrown herself from the leaping place upon the rocks below, before her flesh grew cold.

"When the wearers of this greenstone die, it does not. Keep it always warm, O Huia. Should it ever become cold it would lose its powers of comfort and protection. Never part with it, O Huia. When you need strength refer to it. In this small green tiki dwells the life of your ancestors, your great and illustrious ancestors."

Over her head he places the chain and old Niki fastens it. The warm greenstone settles low on her breast, out of sight beneath her dress. Many of the old ones are weeping and those in the kumara patch with their unerring instinct of communal sympathy bring their tears along too. "Ah . . ." you hear among them.

"I'd better go home now," from Huia. "I always feed Déodonné."

"Let her go," advise the old ones.

When she has gone he says, "I was going to instruct her about the rents." The extras return to the kumara patch.

"Ah . . ." from the old ones. "But she too young, ay."

"The trust is in her name. The Maori Affairs Department in Wellington knows all about it. I'm too tired. But you all know that the Te Renga Renga lands include the whole of the river area except the piece I gave to the Education Department for the school. Harry Dunn's place is leased. As there are so few remaining Te Renga Renga, the income from the rents will not be subjected to inordinate division. The first thing I have arranged for Maori Affairs to do is to repay in full her white people, the Considines, who have brought her up and kept her for twelve years. Eleven, I mean. Is it eleven?"

"About that, ay, Humpty, he should know. He got it in the book, her birth."

"There's a large sum earmarked for Richmond Considine."

"Ah . . ." Agreement.

"And another thing. This must be watched. Huia is the future rangatira of the Te Renga Renga but her name is not Te Renga Renga. Her father's marriage to my granddaughter Kaa was valid. You were there yourselves. Her name is Huia Brice Considine. It was registered in Humpty's books. He is the registrar of births and deaths, and of marriages. The marriage was not registered, since it was not performed in the pakeha legal code, but the birth was. Take good note of that."

"Ah . . ." is all they say.

"As you know, Memory and Sire are servants of the Te Renga Renga. They must serve Huia when she is older and needs it. Whakaturia is a body servant of Huia's and must remain within call. Togi is to supervise her life—and care for her always. I am very tired."

"Where do you want her to be educated?"

"She was booked in at Hukarere at birth."

Old Niki removes her pipe, "Now look, O Koro. These white people, Considine, they go, ay, when they gets paid? And what going to happen to our girl then?"

"Our girl stays. And remember that. She goes to Hukarere Maori Girls' College and not with the Considines. She has already drunk the strength of the white man and quite enough blood of the white man. So now . . . finish."

"One more thing, O Koro. This Huia she a puhi, to be untouched by man until given in tribal alliance. That right?"

"Enough now . . . my sitting-bones are aching."

"O Koro—the Whakaangiangi down-river they wants our Huia in tribal alliance for their young Mita."

" 'Let these remaining days be mine. I . . .' "

"You hang on, O Koro," from Niki. "You know what you jus' say? You say our Huia she drink quite enough bloods of the white man. Time she marry Maori, ay? This kid she three-quarter white now. Time she marry Maori, O Koro." The pipe remains out.

"Ah . . . it would be a great relief. All this white culture she has in her blood . . . it's time it came back to the Maori. But I'm so weary. Get this over. See to these things. Watch Huia Brice Considine's name. Fix up the payment to the Considine tribe. 'Let the small basket of the wayfarer be filled.' Now talk no more to me about these matters. They belong to

143

the future and I am of the past. 'Let these remaining days be mine; I am like the declining sun, a tree fallen in the flood waters.' "

Huia leaves the grave of her mother beneath the poplar at the back of That Side pa and hastens to the riverbank. Recrossing the river with Memory and them, Memory chattering away nonstop of his own magnificent prowess with a boar in the forest, Huia takes up a second paddle although one is quite enough. "O Memory," in Maori, "on high thy paddle.
"For the plunge, poise.
To the landing, the canoe.
Hurry, thou, hurry."

THE summer holidays will be here in a few weeks but children don't see far ahead. The great big living pulsing enveloping *now* consumes them most of the time. The little group kissing Puppa goodbye at the back door in the morning before leaving for school . . . they know no more than that they are kissing Puppa and the baby girl goodbye in the morning. Yet this tableau framed in the doorway . . . Puppa poised on his crutches with Déodonné standing beside him with her hand in his, is destined to follow them in mind till the very end of their days. The two of them are so utterly and terribly defenseless. What makes it so unbearable is that these two seem so happy, as their protectors move off down the path, as they pad barefoot down the trodden path, the path through the foxgloves with a curve in it.

When Mumma and the children reach the lane they stop and look back upon them, at this unforgettable picture. It seems to Huia that never, up-, down- or across-river, up, down or across creation, could there be a more elegant gentleman, and the music ever-present in her mind becomes the song that is so indivisibly a part of him: "By the side of a murmuring stream. An elegant gentleman sat . . ." so that she waits behind the others a moment before she too turns away.

She follows along behind on her own, falling farther and farther back. The lane curls down to the water's edge to what they call Puppa's corner, then in sheer coquetry winds up and away again until it loiters beneath the high bluff known as the leaping place of Tikawe, from which her ancestor Tikawe Hine had thrown her seductive body upon the rocks below, greenstone tiki and all. And all because of "a love."

Huia loiters here too, trying to fathom the meaning of "a love" over which one could throw oneself from the top of a cliff upon the sharp rocks below. On the

145

face of the cliff spurts the thousand-jacket suffusing the morning with fragrance. It is told in This Side that if you hold a finger of its frothy blossoms between your nose and mouth you will think of "a love." But when she does this, who should appear before her inner eye but Mita of the Whakaangiangi down-river . . . his brown face, his midnight eyes, his perfect college English and his smart modern ways.

But Huia is not yet ready to blush. There is in her no more than a vague premonition of awakening, like a sleeper stirring before dawn. She knows only that she does not want to drop the thousand-jacket, and she fixes it in her hair. How should she know that in just this way the women of her tribe for generations back wore thousand-jacket in their hair? Her ancestor Tikawe Hine herself, who lived at the top of this bluff a hundred years ago, fancied the thousand-jacket and thrilled to the same scent.

After school, she resolves—already having forgotten the tableau in the doorway—I'll go across-river to That Side and ask the old one to tell me all about Tikawe. Consciously her fingers seek the greenstone warm beneath her dress—the ornament that knew the rocks below.

The great lord of life, the sun, has not yet retired behind the western rim when she returns across the

146

water to This Side where she finds the rest of the children still swimming—Flower's mother, too, who loves the water, ducking her head like a taniwha. But soon she gets out and dresses to return to the school to give piano lessons. Huia rounds up the others professionally—they should all have returned to Puppa by now. At this moment as they make their way up the flowered roadway to the corner Huia desperately loves them all.

Holding Clarendon's hand on one side and Richmond's on the other, with Simon and Trelawny pressing near, she begins on the loveliest story: not about her ancestor Tikawe, since they're not fond of Maori stories, but about something that interests them glamorously—all about when she gets her rents when the old one has died; she tells them with all the drama she can lay her tongue to how Daniel and Hamish have already found the grand house with balconies and balustrades and at least two staircases on the other side of the North Island in Tauranga by the sea, where, although there is no forest and hardly any rain, there are still plenty of flowers.

It turns out that in their future life they will all wear velvet clothes like Eva Dunn, white shoes and socks like the children of the guests, ride glossy Arab steeds with manes and tails that practically sweep the ground, and even a new mother appears with hair as gold as a cloud at sunset, eyes as blue as these very

147

daisies right here at their feet and a voice like the murmur of a stream at midnight. In short this new mother will be exactly like the guest who comes and leans on Puppa's windowsill at times, shaded by the tree. "Just like Miss Eglantine. But that's not all. . . ."

"What else?"

The departed sun has left behind him trails and swirls and bunches of sky-blossom and the moment of magic approaches. "Guess what we'll see when we get home?"

"What?"

"Know what we'll see? Guess."

"What, Huia, what?"

"We'll see Puppa *walking*."

"We'll see Puppa walking. We'll see Puppa walking. Hurray, hurray, hurray."

Suddenly they run in the twilight of miracle up the lane to the clearing where, at the sight of the yellow window, they whirl into the brightest dancing.

Spinning and dipping down the path Huia thinks she can hear beneath the voices of the others Puppa's voice at the back door. She remembers the tableau at the door this morning of a most elegant gentleman. At the back door? Then it's true he is walking. He has come out straight and tall to surprise them and because he must be lonely without Flower's mother at home. In the dusk they smell the browning potatoes

148

but cannot see the horse. Calling and dancing down the path, all they can think of is Puppa in the doorway, new, tall, unlocked, his hair and mustache brushed in that civilized way . . . an exceedingly elegant gentleman.

And sure enough here he is in the doorway, but not upright as they had thought . . . indeed he's not standing at all. As they fly dancing nearer they find him struggling dangerously down the steps on his crutches and shouting to God for mercy with Déodonné crying behind him. And they see the Dunn beating him with a piece of wood and there is blood on his face, so that in no way is he elegant after all.

THE tui is not exactly a black bird though you hear him described that way. Actually there's a sheen on his back much like the interior of a paua shell picked up on the rocks by the sea—a miniature rainbow in disarray. One movement you see green, the next you see purple, whichever way he turns himself, flashing to the light. When you see Tui swaying and preening in the sheerest exhibitionism you know what iridescence means—as when you hold a paua in your hand, again you know iridescence.

The paua eyes in the carving of Tane Mahuta in the forgotten dwelling place gleam beyond Huia as she stands beneath him. She traces his grotesque features with a finger as she thinks about him. "O Togi," in Maori, "the forest god has a woman here. Who is she? Look, he's lifting her up."

"That's his wife, O Huia." It is late Sunday afternoon and he has put away his guests and boats. He is sitting on the earth floor against the holding-up post in his captain's suit and hat.

"Is this the earth-maid my koro told about in a chant?"

"You remember that chant, O Huia?"

" 'Desired Tane Mahuta a wife.

Formed he a woman-shape from the earth,

Lay he his body upon it,

Breathed he his life into it.

Rose the earth-formed shape, a maid.'

"But he tells me these things in hard chants. If he were Puppa he would tell a story."

"Me too," he says.

The next thing she is on the ground also with both hands on his knees. His mature eyes penetrate hers but she has not reached the blushing time yet. Her wide eyes like canoes tethered at an angle take him aboard in innocence. Neither does his gaze waver as he speaks in Maori, "A very long time ago, taku aroha, there was a being called Tane Mahuta. He was the god of the forest and the birds and of all the forest creatures. He was of radiant appearance; lightning flashed from his armpits and he was girdled with rainbow. But at that time creation was not complete. Not only were there no people yet on the earth but there were no goddesses either.

"So one day when Tane was feeling the need of a wife, alone up there in the heavens, he ungirdled his rainbow, threw one end down to earth and descended. Taking soft clay from the riverbed he shaped from it a woman. He made it as lifelike as possible and all that he felt a woman's body should be; slender as the Dawn Maid dispensing her light, eyes like canoes tethered at an angle and with legs that could run, climb, swim, sway and have a love should she wish it. Yet when he had finished she remained on the ground motionless and colorless. 'My wife has no life,' he pondered, 'yet I have enough for two.'

"Stirred by a strange new impulse which he had not experienced before, he lay his body full length upon the clay form, his feet to her feet, his mouth to hers, for the whole of the afternoon. By the time twilight came his own bodily warmth had entered the clay form beneath him and into the throat he had made he breathed his own breath. A wonderful change began taking place; the hair took on the blackness of the night with the sheen of the tui's back, the eyes showed the depth of the water in the river and the form stirred beneath him. Tane stood and raised her to her feet. He took the new warm hand and led her into the forest to the base of the rainbow, the lightning flashing more brightly from his armpits, and together they began climbing it and as they mounted he chanted:

> To the first heaven,
> To the second heaven,

To the third heaven,
To the fourth heaven,

To the fifth heaven,
To the sixth heaven,
To the seventh heaven,
To the eighth heaven,
To the ninth heaven,
To the tenth heaven.

"There in the land of the gods, the tenth heaven, Tane lay upon her again but this time did not rise until the Dawn Maid stepped over the eastern horizon dispensing her nuptial light. And from these two, Tane Mahuta and his earth-formed maid, was born the first man—the first being wholly mortal."

"His name was Tiki," from Huia.

"You remember, taku aroha."

A sigh and a stretch from Huia and she rolls on the ground before him. "O Togi . . . I'd like to go to the tenth heaven. Would Tane Mahuta take me?"

"He has been known to descend his rainbow when he sees below him bathing in the river some lovely Maori maiden and have a love with her, but he doesn't take her to the tenth heaven. There the gods do not die, but a mortal maiden would and her corpse would defile their land."

"I've never seen him."

"Ah, that's just it, taku aroha. He does not reveal himself to mortals—he changes into the form of a mortal man himself. You want to look out, ay, Huia? You never know when a man he might be a god." He's back in English now.

"I'd rather marry a man who was really a god than just a real boy like Mita."

"But he doesen' stay an' then you gets lonely. A man who is a god he doesen' stay. All you gets out of it that's a kid."

Huia gets up and takes herself back to the carving of Tane and his earth-maid and traces the grooves with a finger. "Puppa told us a story about a dark-haired princess who was in the forest and she married an invisible god."

"He did?"

"But he didn't finish that story ever."

"You ask him to finish this story?"

"Often I have, but he said, 'The future will finish it.' But I don't know the future. I don't know where to go and find the future to finish it for me."

THE midsummer holidays pulse by uncounted in the clearing but severely ticked off by time, as accu-

154

rately as though by a landlord. Trelawny is ready for high school this year except that Mumma can't get any of the big ones to sponsor him, neither Daniel, Hamish, Rose nor May. How could Hamish take Trelawny after missing Flower? The only thing for him is another horse to make the daily journey with Sue, or a secondhand bike. The boy must be educated, whatever his ways.

"Sue," opens Mumma respectfully one morning, peering in the back room, "would you get me some wood, dear? There's a pile of clothes in the washhouse that would shame This Side House." Puppa is sitting at the table in the kitchen solemnly washing the dishes, giving them the whole of his creative attention like an artist at his canvas.

"Oh, Mumma, I'm learning my history. Make Lance do it." He is home for the holidays. "He's not doing anything."

Mumma brushes back her hair with an arm, since her hands are wet, and walks through the house to the front room where Lance is huddled over some wonderful wheels and screws. "Lance," she addresses his shoulders, "you'll get me some wood, won't you?" She usually approaches the males of the family with instinctive awe. "I'm held up with the washing."

"Oh, Mumma, I'm busy. What happened to that enormous pile of wood that Daniel got? Chopped and everything? I can't get the wood. I've been trying to

155

make this engine go ever since I came home. Make Trelawny do it. He's not doing anything."

From the rusty trusty old grand in the kitchen where Huia is practicing shoots a careering cadenza not unlike the squeal of one of Tane's creatures caught in the talons of a hawk. Baby whines an obbligato on the floor while from Puppa at the dishes the sound effects, click-clack-click.

Trelawny is lying on his back on the grass, far from doing nothing; he is industriously absorbing the morning. A piece of sweet grass stalk is between his lips, a knee sways idly to the music and he watches the blue sky—his eyes are full of the blue. "Trelawny," says Mumma with genuine affection, "would you get me a little wood, dear? I must get this washing on the line before a shower comes. There's a good boy."

"Oh, Mumma, I'm tired."

"But you'd get some wood for your mother."

"Wait till I've finished being tired. Make Simon get it. He's not doing anything."

Simon is turning out to be an active and creative person and already there are two bids from the big ones in the outside world to take Simon the moment he has qualified for high school. True, he has not Puppa's beautiful face as Trelawny has, but his personality is acceptable. At the moment he's building himself a magnificent house of manuka brush not far off. "Simon," with purpose, "I want you to get me

156

some wood. Come and get some wood for your poor mother."

"No," flat. "Make Huia do it. She's not doing anything." To prove the contrary a cascade of semiquavers showers like a waterfall from the top of the keyboard to fall bubbling into a pool in the bass.

Mumma sways back to the kitchen and says to the streak at the piano engaged in this tough allegro. "Huia—" she has to speak in her ear—"you're different from the others. *You'll* get some wood when I ask you."

"Oh, Flower's mother," the hands do not pause, "you've always said that if anyone were practicing they were not to be disturbed. Make that great big lazy Lance do it. He's not practicing."

Voice rising, "But I've asked him already."

Hands pause, "Well what about that Richmond out there? He *never* does anything." Click on clack from Puppa's dishes.

Back to the front door again. "Richmond—" he is building with Simon—"go and get your poor mother some wood."

"Oh, Mumma, you know I'm too little to get the wood." Nevertheless he heaves a large branch of manuka into position on the house they are building. "You know I am only a baby. Make someone else do it."

The tactical patience gives out. "There's no one else

except Clarendon and the baby." Richmond examines the two little girls in a new light, from another point of view. "Clarrie could get some very little wee tiny wood, couldn't she?"

Mumma sways swiftly back to the kitchen, the river lapping at its banks. "Richie, Richie, they won't get the wood. All these children and not a stick of wood. And me trying to do the washing."

Puppa pauses and straightens his thin shoulders. Ominously, "Won't they get the wood, Mary?" A roar of music from the piano in the bass like the sound of boulders on the bed of the river when the current is high, bumping and crashing upon one another.

"They won't get the wood. They won't get the wood."

"They won't?" in routine amazement. "By the living God, if I could walk I'd make them get the wood." The stroke of a hammer on steel from Lance, the voices of Simon and Richmond building their house, a soft artistic bawling from Trelawny sprawling on the grass, the whish of a page turning over in Sue's book, and from the rattling old grand rises an ascending chromatic passage like the shriek of a wild cuckoo.

Mumma's voice ascends with the chromatic and the shriek of an actual cuckoo practicing in the puriri. "They won't get the wood, they won't get the wood. What'll I do? What'll I do? All these children and I've got no wood. And me slaving day and night to bring them up decently. And look at the way they treat their poor mother. Their poor overworked mother." All this directed at Puppa.

His frail body stiffens. He puts down his dishcloth, fumbles for his crutches and jerks himself to his feet, trembling with rage. His voice starts at a shout that terrifies the cuckoo, who takes off smartly for the entire morning to avoid getting the wood himself. He starts shouting to those at the top of the family far in the outside world from sheer established habit, and I wouldn't be surprised if they heard him. "Daniel, Hamish, Rose, God damn it. May, Flower, Susanna, God curse it. Lance, Trelawny . . . Simon, Huia . . . Richmond, Clarendon, Déodonné. *Anyone* at all. Get your mother some wood." But only the keyboard replies as the chromatic reaching its treble zenith explodes at the top of the keyboard in a shower and spray of waterdrops descending in trills to the minor.

"Am I not master of my own house?" In his passion he fails to grip his crutches. "Can no one hear me? Will no one obey me? Who am I but 'only the father'? by the living God, if I could walk I'd make you all obey me." Swaying with emotion he loses a crutch and falls back on his chair.

The allegro gives way to a wary andante, the voices outside lower, baby stops whining, Trelawny soft-pedals his bawling, the sound of the hammer decreases somewhat while from the back room a page turns over.

Mumma's feet draw astride, her fingers contract and she looks up through the ceiling to some vision she perceives there, her eyes rolling upward showing the unquenchable passion in her. In a sepulchral voice, "I'll thrash them till I break every bone in their bodies. I'll flog them till they scream for mercy." Down goes her head and she charges.

There's a scuffling sort of sound in the whare, a kind of scattering sound and all at once the place is empty. But Mumma is an excellent runner, inadvertently fit, and here's this scene in the clearing of children and fowls, cats and horses flying like leaves before the wind of vengeance . . . in and out of the stumps and over the logs. Birds take off in high-flying flocks as they do in the migrating season, furred and feathered creatures of Tane squeal off in panic as several of the children floundering in the foxgloves are caught. Down come one pair of pants after the other —smack-smack-smack from the roughened hand until the clearing has the character of London in wartime with every siren screaming for mercy.

In time Mumma returns to the house puffing with satisfaction, wiping her hands on the back of her dress. "That'll teach the little fiends a lesson. That'll teach them how to treat their mother."

Sue strolls out from the back room surprised, open

160

book in hand, "What's all that fearful noise outside? I thought there was harmony in the house. What's been happening?"

Mumma pulls up mid-kitchen, awe and pride suffusing her face, and whispers, "I've just chased a princess out of the house."

Suddenly she opens her mouth, throws back her head and screeches and screeches with laughter. Puppa's mustache quivers a moment, then here are these rows of falsetto notes joining Mumma's shrieks until baby on the floor starts laughing too.

In time, not too long, there is a certain congestion at the wood heap; Huia drags along great branches, Lance tries his hand on the ax, Simon and Richmond cart it in, sniffing with a showy poignancy, while Clarrie brings in the chips. Sue of course returns to her book, when she can see the show is over, picking up again where she knows she left off, and everyone else does too. Puppa gets on with the dishes and Mumma with the washing.

A BENIGN autumn evening.

The children run down the up-river lane, sent to bring the mail, leaving the baby girls with Puppa, since Mumma is digging up a patch to put in winter cabbages and a few rows of potatoes. But Puppa is still all right, even so, since there's a guest beneath the puriri tree leaning on his sill. Mumma doesn't seem to mind the guests, recalling as they do the days of past prosperity; the large balconied house and the servants in London and Richmond glamorously walking. What an upright tall man he was then and such a spring in his step. 'F course, then, even as he does now, he would stand in the middle of the house on occasion at the foot of the stairs shouting at the top of his voice so that he could be heard not only to the farthest corner but out in the street as well. And he broke the dishes then too but far better than he breaks them now. At that time he could actually *throw* the plates magnificently to the ceiling during any given meal if some scrounging fifth-rate hack of a journalist gave him a bad review. The only time he didn't shout and smash every dish upon the table was during the sensational court case when his books were banned. An astounding hush on the home that time until the summer day when they found him no longer there.

The children skip and dance down the lane in and out of the trees and along the riverbank with not a care upon them. Not only is there a guest with Puppa, removing their responsibility, but it's a woman this time. Paul Dunn said that her name had not been on the list in the paper when a liner berthed recently, which means nothing at all to the children, since she has given them each a *shilling*—an enormous sum in the clearing. Not that Puppa is in any way impressed; he's often irritable after the visit of this particular guest and smokes his pipe furiously. "The first sin in this life is to be boring," he states, "and the second is to be bored."

But the children recall none of this as they skip, kicking up the soft summer dust, leaving the patterns of their feet in it and calling down the birds; they are as intrinsic a part of the evening as the furred and feathered creatures of Tane. At Puppa's corner they stop and sit and stare in fascination at their wealth. "This is my shilling," from Trelawny. "I'll buy some lollies with it."

From Huia, "It's too good for lollies. This is the very first time Puppa has allowed us to take money from a guest."

"She talks soft," from Richmond.

"Say 'softly,' " from Huia.

"She talks softly then."

"Yes, I'm going to buy some lollies," Trelawny.

"No-o-o . . . Trel."

"What then?"

"Give all the shillings to me and we'll save up for something big."

"Someping big, someping big," from Richmond.

Huia takes Puppa's place on his log, reflects on the

163

river, then presently begins singing, "By the side of a murmuring stream An elegant gentleman sat." Crosses one knee upon the other and folds her hands upon them. Then clears her throat, "God damn it."

A cackle of laughter from the others. Then she lifts her voice in rage, "Who am I in this accursed house? Only the father. Simon, Huia, Richmond, God curse it. Can no one hear me? By the living God, if I could walk I'd make them get the wood," at which the others double up.

At length Trelawny says, "Come on, let's get down to the store before Humpty shuts up."

Huia, "Let's put it all together and save up." Swings a foot. "A wheelchair for Puppa."

Silence. Huia begins digging a hole in the bank.

"You said," from Trelawny, "you said, you said once that when your silly old koro dies and you get your silly old rents that you'd buy Puppa a wheelchair."

Digging, "He won't die for a long time yet. He keeps on nearly dying all the time without stopping and keeps on getting better. I won't mind when he dies. Then I won't have to learn my genealogy. How would you like to have to learn your genealogy from a long way before the migration five hundred years ago?" Digging, "We'll have to buy this wheelchair ourselves."

"What about the fungus? There's a fearful lot of it. It's time to sell it. That'll buy a wheelchair."

"With these shillings it would. We'll sell it to that guest with Puppa, shall we?"

"She might not want fungus."

"She might," still digging.

From Richmond, "What tat hole in the bank for, Hoo-a?"

"A bank to save the money in."

Up they dance and shout, "A bank, a bank to save the money in. A wheelchair for Puppa, hurray, hurray."

A few steps up the road from the bridge is the store. Squat it sits among its verandas like a kuia among her skirts. Roses swing at one end and plums swell at the other while proud tree ferns uncurl their fronds behind. Kuias rest on this veranda on their way up from the landing and smoke rises from the chimney straight up in the air.

By the time the children arrive the boat is puffing up the evening river with the village mail. There's the usual eddying of children about, Maoris appear and disappear in admirable serenity, fashionable guests are taking the air after dinner from the House farther up, young ones meet in furtive love trysts in the shadows of the plums, many dogs and more fowls join the throng, and you hear the guitar down the bank. All facets of This Side are represented, waiting for the mail, yet the store receives them all: through them all, beneath them all she sits among her verandas . . . unperturbed, in spite of them all . . . squat, bland, serene.

Paul Dunn is here for the mail in impeccable clothes, and as he steps from the veranda toward Huia, hands pocketed, he takes in her bare feet, yellow dress and all this furious hair. "I still remember that crack you gave me and I always will."

In fine Mumma style, "How dare you speak to me, you *servant*."

His hands clench and he blushes badly. "I'll speak to you if I want to."

She spits accurately in his face, at which his hands unclench into something like claws, "I'll remember that too."

She turns abruptly and finds Mita of the Whaka-angiangi home from college for the weekend, dressed easily as poshly as Paul. Her fingers seek her green-stone. Humpty in the doorway, who misses nothing, observes to a crony, "And what do I see? I see, I see. I see another go of the ngati Whakaangiangi down-river at a tribal alliance with Te Renga Renga. In my own living memory this has happened before. Make way for the marriage ceremonial."

Mita holds an armful of still twitching eels but he says in college English, "Do you know that song they are singing down the bank, Rangatira?"

"Of course I do."

"Do you know what it means? 'If I were a bird flying I would fly right to your nest. I would embrace your body and you would turn to me; you would turn to me.' "

Huia, brought up on Mumma's version of the facts of life and on Puppa's insubstantial angels, does not blush. But Paul Dunn does. He steps nearer to Mita. "That's a dirty love song. Togi wrote that song for Huia and my dad says fancy a grown man singing a filthy sex song to a girl of twelve. My dad says it's a dirty business and my dad said there would be more to it than a song."

Huia is still no wiser but Mita is about fifteen. For no reason that Huia can see, Mita's fist shoots out. There's a smack, a stiff grunt and a gasp from those about them. Back comes Paul's fist in well-trained style and right here out of nothing there's a fight: a crowd, darting fowls, blood and eels everywhere. . . .

"Here's a go, here's a go," from the crowd.

Humpty materializes, and swiftly summarizes. "Now-now, now-now, what have we here? Stab my stepmother, but didn't I leave the war in France? Oyez, oyez, gather ye near. All right, folks, I'll take your money. On my right the heir to the Dunn for-

167

tune. On my left the Whakaangiangi, the illustrious tribe down-river. Both for the hand of Huia Brice Considine, future rangatira of the ngati Te Renga Renga. Oyez, oyez, gather ye near. Show me your money, folks. . . ."

A guest whispers to him, "Fancy. Two well-dressed boys fighting over a barefoot Maori. Not even a clean dress."

" 'Course, y'see," his voice low, "this Huia is a puhi . . . to be untouched by man until given in tribal alliance in marriage ceremonial. Mita has an eye to his future."

Thud, biff . . . crash . . .

Later, after the younger Paul has staggered off leaving the older Mita lying on the stones crying and bleeding, Humpty confides to his crony, " 'Course, y'see, what the brown joker had was only strength, but the white bloke had technique. What am I uttering— a profound truth? What price the Maori strength against the technique of the white man? 'Through women and land are men lost,' runs a Maori proverb. Huia is both woman and land."

On the way home in the twilight Huia again draws a sprig of thousand-jacket below her nose and as the intoxicating fragrance assails her a physical woman awakes. Something raw and new is happening in her. For one thing she is hot in every area, so surprisingly, even to her scalp. Her feet are hot, her knees as well, along with the rest of her self in her first comprehensive blush; and for another . . . strange fine pains dart in the untouched, unthought-of privacies of her body of which she was unaware. Stabs in the secrecy of the pelvic area link with sensations in the breasts that so far boast no contour, as though these embryonic organs had long recognized each other but only now hailed each other.

A child is clutched by primeval rapture to which she knows but one answer: turning to a shaggy tree trunk she embraces it passionately. She presses her slight person against its bulk and kisses it with ardor until, flung so carelessly on the storm of instinct, she swings into fantastic dancing, calling to the others, "The marriage ceremonial, the marriage ceremonial. See me dance at my marriage ceremonial." Never up, down or across creation could there be a lovelier sight.

By the time the children mount the lane with what must be called the mail, the usual anxiety for Puppa strikes them. There along the path is the square of yellow light in the gloom. True, they have only been for the mail but they have lived through several lifetimes, and their kind of living takes time. But no one will say, "Where have you been?" or "You must not be so late."

Clambering in over the sill they find Puppa sitting

169

by the stove, hair and mustache brushed, and singing
to the babies at his knee a strange little English song
they have not heard before.

Oh, going down the river in the old steam boat,
Yippai yippai, yippai yippai, yippai yippai day.
Going down the river in the old steam boat,
Yippai yippai, yippai yippai day.
Farewell, farewell. Farewell Miss Fanny Vane.
I'm off in the Indiana
To see my Susianna
And to catch the morning trai—ai—n.

IT is toward the end of this autumn when the
children notice a new pile of diapers growing for the
poor little, dear little Beljuns—although Huia knows
better by now—as well as an extraordinary pile of
wood growing outside that Mumma drags tirelessly up
from the river whenever she goes there swimming—
also when she does not—against the time when she
will no longer be able.

But it is well into winter with the forest out of sight
behind the swinging rain curtains and the river howling in flood when Mumma, heaving herself home

from school with the little ones trailing and bawling behind her, her turned-out toes sodden with mud and her skirt fringed with it, with the weight of her parcels and of her own body calling for many a stop and thinking of the cup of tea that Puppa will make her— it is in winter when, arriving in the clearing, she discovers that the Dunn has sledged away all her wood, systematically in lieu of rent.

True, as they hear later, Puppa himself struggled down the back step and tried to prevent him, at the top of his voice laying upon the Dunn the richest of English curses, upon him and all his descendants forever, in the most exotic language, but Mumma still cries like anything on her chair at the table and nothing and no one are able to stop her, even Puppa's very best jokes and Huia's best acting. She speaks but two single words, "The cur."

And later in the evening the sorrowing children find her lying on the floor in the bedroom crying and trembling and groaning so much that Humpty has to borrow someone else's sledge and bring her down to the landing in the middle of the night, where Togi takes her away down-stream on the flooded river to the hospital at Whanganui and Flower has to come home to mind them. For Flower is only at high school whereas the big ones are either married like Daniel, mid-university like Hamish, mid-nursing training like Rose or mid-concert tour like May. True, Flower herself will soon be mid-stage training but that time is not quite yet. For a while she can train on the stage in the clearing.

Flower is nearly seventeen now and here is all this glory of shining green eyes, shining brown curls, shining teeth, shining love and shining personality dropped back on the stage in the whare. Why should it take tragedy to restore to the flock the brightest-blooming blossom o' it?

The handle of my steering paddle thrills to action,
My paddle named Kautu-ki-te-rangi.
It guides to the horizon but dimly discerned,
The horizon that lifts before me,
The horizon that ever draws near,
The horizon that ever recedes,
The horizon that causes doubt,
The horizon that instills dread,
The horizon with unknown power,
The horizon not hitherto pierced.
The lowering skies above,
The raging seas below
Oppose the untraced path
My ship must go.

The handle of my steering paddle thrills to action,
My paddle named Kautu-ki-te-rangi. . . .

     —Paddle song of the Aotea Canoe
      (fourteenth century)

IT is not till midsummer during Christmas holidays, when the blooms of the foxgloves opening in succession up their stalks have reached the tips, that the children return from the mail with a letter from their mother to Flower. They don't dance down the clearing as they are fond of doing but climb disconsolately over the sill and sit in various places: on the woodbox, on the form, on the bed in the corner, on the sack at the hearth, on the sill and in the tree. Excepting Flower, who sits in her mother's chair at the side of the table, turning to Puppa at the end.

There's an unfamiliar tone in the room. Flower leans back in her chair, her hands palms upward in the way of her mother and her eyes holding that rare softness that would come to her mother's when the sun redness broke through the rain mat to the west.

Puppa pours the milk into the two cups and turns to the teapot. With both hands and some risk he tips it enough to pour the tea, then, taking both his crutches to get up, replaces one cup, lifts the other precariously from its saucer, crutches dangerously the distance to Flower, delivers the tea and without a word returns.

Flower remains looking out the window and sniffs, that same sniff of courage of her mother's when failing in her assault on life. "Well," she says, brushing back her hair with a forearm, like Mumma, "There y'are, y'see. That's y'curses for you."

Puppa clears his throat and opens his mouth but no comforting remark comes so he sips his tea instead and makes do with, "So she's not coming home yet."

In superb impersonation from Flower comes the Dunn's voice, "An' wot's y'uppishness goin' t'do for ya? It don't bring in a penny. D'y'think I don't get enough of this uppishness in me own This Side House from all these lah-de-dah crowds? An' me keepin' a family an' kids of the gentry on me own land an' nothin' in return. Think y'are goin' to feed off one of y'servants, do ya? I'm not y'servant now. This ain't the past, it's the present. Ya bloody good-for-nothin' toffs with not a penny to y'names. You come down and take on me laundry, Mrs. Considine, an' earn the food an' the wood an' the shelter I let you have off the land I lease. I'm not y'servant now. I'm y'landlord. Can't y'get that into y'bloody heads?"

But no screams of laughter from the children and none rolls on the floor with mirth as they do when

176

Flower starts. The silence is worse, if anything. "Yet," from Sue, "there must be some good in him since he sledged back all the wood again the very next morning and sent a man to chop it."

Puppa says, "It took tragedy to bring him to the realization of his own enormity."

Flower uses a voice that is neither Mumma's nor the landlord's—the voice is her own and all it turns out to be is the whimper of a girl. "It remains that dreadful servant who drove our mother away."

"God bless her," from Puppa.

Flower herself is the only mother Huia has ever known, and at her weeping, Huia's canoe-eyes darken in the way of the rangatiras of the past and to her come words habitually used by generations departed:

"O Flower Ella Considine, I'll avenge your tears one day."

Flower drinks her tea, rises with a sigh and stands a moment. Again she looks through the window as though she expected to see Mumma swaying down the path with her parcels but turns in resignation. "Oh well," she says, "I'd better get a little wood."

"There's plenty and plenty of wood," from Simon. "I chopped a *huge* stack today."

"Let her," from Sue. "Mumma always did something like that when she was upset."

In a moment however they hear Flower's courageous sniffing change to crying. Huia flies out, takes the ax from her, brings her back to the kitchen and strokes her hair. "Puppa," she orders, "tell us a story."

Puppa clears his throat with the best of intentions but nothing whatever comes. He tries changing the position of his hands over and over but still not a word arrives.

"Go on, Puppa. 'Once upon a time . . .' "

Still the unproductive throat-clearing and hand-changing until Huia herself takes center stage and shakes back some of her hair. "Once upon a time there was, there was . . . I mean . . . see? It was one of my ancestors. It was Tikawe Hine. Well she, well she . . . you sit down here, Flow." She sits Flower on her chair and kneels before her. The fire is sparking and the others leave their form, corner bed, sill and tree and gather round the two. "See, this Tikawe was a puhi. That means she was of rangatira blood, to be untouched by man until given in marriage ceremonial for tribal alliance.

"She lived in a fortified pa on the top of that bluff, the leaping place, down the lane. Right up on top of that cliff where you can't see. That's where she lived.

"Now one day Tikawe was given in marriage to a young chieftain of the up-river tribe . . . that's how I come to be related to that tribe up the river. And for some years they lived very happily together and had several sweet children. But one day . . ." Flower is cheering up . . . "her husband climbed down the

178

path to the river and, saying he would be back soon, kissed her goodbye, got into his canoe and paddled away down-river.

"For a long time Tikawe stood on the top of the bluff watching him until his canoe disappeared round a bend, then sadly she returned to her children.

"Many moons she waited. Every day she would go to the clifftop to look along the water but only disappointment awaited her. He did not come. However there dawned a day when someone else came. It was a warrior of my own tribe, Te Renga Renga, and he told Tikawe that her husband was living with another woman on the east coast.

"That night the tribal leaders talked it over in the meeting house but Tikawe remained in her dwelling place. The night long she wept with grief and scorned love and—as is the way in grief—she tore her breast and arms with obsidian flake until the mats reddened about her.

"But when morning came she rose and dressed herself in her finest garments: her kaiteke with the taniko border and the korowai she had woven with her own hands. On her breast was this very greenstone—see?" She draws it from beneath her dress. "The greenstone Takarangi. And in her hair were huia feathers.

"Then, just as the Mist Maiden rose from the river and the birds were tuning up for the day, she walked from her dwelling place to the center of the marae where her people were gathered at their morning meal, and drawing her garments about her and bowing her head she chanted. For some time this chant told of the unfaithfulness of her dear one and of the dishonor that had fallen upon her, until lifting her eyes she gazed at the beauty of the land about her, at the river, the forest and the flowers, and she spoke:

"In my hair the huia plume,
Upon me these fine flaxen cloaks,
Comely the land I look upon.
Red the bloom of the rata vine
And beautiful the calm face of the river
Yet gaze I now my last.

Shall approach me no more any man.
Shall entice no more my body.
Desolate, I, as the river in winter.
In my heart . . . bitterness.
Aue . . . aue . . . aue! . . ."

"Calmly she walked to the edge of the bluff and with a long look down-river where she had last seen her husband she dropped over upon the rocks below. And th-that is the real name of that bluff: the Leaping Place of Tikawe."

"Did she die?" from Richmond sepulchrally.

"Die?" from Clarrie.

"Is her body still there?" from Simon. "Is that true?"

"It is all true. My koro said so. Her bones are in a cave in that cliff—we walk beneath them every day. A-and there's a carved panel of her in the forgotten meeting house covered with spiderweb and moss. I often try to clean it when I go there."

"You said, you said," from Trelawny, "that you Maoris go to Hawaiki when you die."

"Her spirit is in Hawaiki. She's waiting to greet me there. She had a wear of my greenstone once."

"Yes," from Flower, "but what happened to the children?"

"Sue," from Puppa, "you're a girl for books. I've noticed the way you hold a book. You take this key and go to that black box of mine and . . ."

Although it is not real story time no one can stand Flower in this state. Simon puts more wood on the fire, Huia picks up the new baby; Trelawny—believe it or not—picks up the old baby, Clarendon, and Puppa gets to his chair by the window. In no time all are in story formation, on the sill and in the tree. When Sue brings the manuscript Puppa opens it and reads:

"Once upon a time there was a king who was reasonable enough as kings go: he tried not to demand too much of the best from his courtiers and faithfully kept the population in check by frequent 'heads-off' ceremonies. However he was incurably appreciative of beauty, and one day in winter when he was depressed at the bareness about him he let himself go and demanded of his courtiers that he be brought the most beautiful thing in his kingdom. Indeed so strongly did he feel about this that he crashed his scepter on the throne-room floor and declared that the successful courtier should have the hand of his daughter in marriage, whereas those who failed to reach a certain aesthetic standard would most bloodily lose their heads.

"The courtiers—who had already had considerable experience in raking the kingdom for something or other—remained calm, did not panic and set off routinely enough. After all, they argued, the best must be *somewhere* and it was no more than a matter of finding it, at least pretending they had found it, or as a last resort, of persuading the wise men to agree they had found it. As for the heads-off, heads-on issue, didn't everyone know it was a good king's responsibility to balance the birth and death rates?

"So, after the right length of time away, the searchers began returning to the palace with quite a creditable range of beautiful things running from gems and robes through bewitching scents to many a verse and song, all hoping to win the reward of the king's exclusive daughter, but the king reported no relief. Indeed, being far too sensitive a soul to be robust, he felt the strain of disappointment to the point of illness, so that he was obliged to consult his favorite queen.

" 'My dear,' he complained. 'I am forced to the conclusion that my kingdom is, in fact, as mediocre a place as my neighboring monarchs declare. Oh,' he moaned, thumping the floor with his scepter and looking desperately out the window into the palace gardens where a lone bird sat on a bare branch, 'how ugliness offends me.'

"The queen mopped her eyes in routine sympathy. 'You must consult your wise men, Your Majesty.'

"In his stress the king cut the matter short and sent for the wisest of all the wise men.

"In due course, a bit late, actually, having been held up on the way to the palace by the crowds attending the 'heads-off' ceremonies, the wisest man finally arrived and was received by the king in his thinking room. Three times the wise man bowed to the floor before his sovereign, then, gazing enraptured out the window at the design of the still bird on the branch set in the silver rain, he pronounced absently, 'Peace be upon Your Majesty.'

" 'Peace,' thundered the king. 'How can you mention peace? I am the most frustrated man in my kingdom.'

"The wisest man, who was notorious for his ruthlessness in coming to the point, asked, 'Why, what is your problem?'

183

" 'I want beauty,' roared the king. 'Here am I, a man of the most delicate taste and the keenest sensibility surrounded by the gross and the ordinary. Yes, the banal and the mediocre. The—the . . . pray, *look* at me, sir,' he bellowed.

"Guiltily the wisest man looked up from admiring the palace cat washing her face at his feet.

" 'As I was saying,' whined the king, 'to such a state of profoundest melancholy have my surroundings reduced me that only the sight of something extraordinarily lovely could possibly re-establish my . . . my . . .'

" 'What,' cut in the other, 'does Your Majesty mean by beauty?'

" 'By my crown and scepter, sir, do you suggest that a man with my record, of my renown, a sheer prince of aesthetics, does not know the meaning of beauty? I who suffer so continuously from the . . . from the . . . by the Prophet, sir,' he bawled, crashing his scepter on the thinking-room floor so that it broke in several pieces, '*will* you attend to me?'

"The wisest man, gazing fascinated at the sand running through the golden hourglass, jumped and clasped his hands in attention.

" 'As I was saying,' thundered the king. 'In the name of Allah, what was I saying?'

" 'You were telling me, sire, what you knew of beauty.'

" 'Was I *indeed?*'

" 'Your Majesty was saying that beauty was not wholly of tangible form; you said beauty is an emotion rather—a sensuous response to natural form.'

" 'Ah . . . exactly, sir. Exactly. That's me all over.'

" 'Your Majesty was saying that the form which has this appeal to the senses may occur in anything that is seen, heard, smelled, tasted, touched or felt. Yet even in this comprehensive field is not found the *most* beautiful thing in your or anyone else's kingdom—not specifically. It is found both in a kingdom and beyond kingdoms.'

" 'Do you dare to tell me . . .'

" 'Your Majesty interrupts.'

" 'By my scepter—' he looked round for it—'I'll have you beheaded for your insolence.'

"At the mention of his head the wise man at last took an active interest in the conversation. 'Would you then remove the one head holding the knowledge required for your royal relief?'

"The King lowered his own head, almost losing his crown. With a catch in his voice, 'Proceed, sir.'

"The other, gazing absently at the sand running through the hourglass, said, 'The most beautiful thing in the world is without number and everywhere.'

" 'I don't understand.'

" 'You interrupt again.'

"A protesting noise squeezed from the king but he stuffed his beard in his mouth, and the other continued, 'It is without number and all about you.'

" 'Tell me, oh, tell me," groaned the king, 'and anything you ask shall be granted. Even the hand of my daughter.'

"The other mildly stroked his beard. 'A small request does occur to me.'

" 'It shall be granted. Name this elusive, exclusive thing and by my scepter—' he recovers a piece of it from the floor and flings it at the cat—'it shall be granted if it costs every head at court. Attend to me, sir,' he shouts at the other, who is pacifying pussy, then whispers, 'Proceed, sir, please.'

" 'What was it we were discussing again?'

" 'We were discussing the most beautiful thing in the world.' Then, with a humility never before witnessed in the thinking room, 'I am listening, sir.'

" 'Your Majesty's bearing in the presence of wisdom is at last seemly. Even I, the wisest of all wise men, am humble in the presence of wisdom.'

" 'I am listening.'

"A moment of silence in the thinking room, then the wisest man, his eyes on the running sand, spoke. 'The most beautiful thing can only be known. It is . . .' his eyes on the running sand . . . 'a moment of time.'

186

"By the side of a murmuring stream . . ."

"You haven't finished," from the floor.

"An elegant gentleman sat . . ."

"That's not the end," from the sill.

"It's the aesthetic end."

"What does that mean?" from a branch in the tree.

"It means there's a natural dip in the rhythm there. The beat is complete. The story moment is over. On the top of his head was his wig . . ."

"But you didn't say what the wisest man's small request was."

"Neither I did. I didn't write that."

"Well, hurry up, what was it?"

"He—aa . . ." lays down the manuscript . . . "After a lengthy discussion, and at times heated, on the character of a moment of time, during which the king forgot all about his crown and scepter, the wisest man said, 'Now, old fellow, there is that little matter of my request.'

" 'Name it, brother.'

" 'I beg that I be spared the reward of your daughter.' Then he got out as fast as he could.

"On the top of his head was his wig . . ."

"Did he get his head chopped off for insolence?"

"On the top of his wig was his hat . . ."

"But how," from Sue, "can we recognize wisdom so we can be humble before it? I'd like to be humble, Puppa."

"On the top of his wig was his hat, hat, ha-a-a-a . . ."

"What," from Huia, "is a moment of time?"

". . . a-a-a-at. On the top of his wig was his *hat*."

Pass on, O Sire, along the quiet ways,
The beloved of my heart, my shelter and defense
Against the bleak south wind.
My speaking-bird that charmed the assembled tribes,
That swayed the people's councils.

Clothe him, the Father, with the stately garments,
The very fine cloaks Tahu-whenua and Taharangi;
Place in his ear the precious jewel-stone,
The greenstone Kahurangi,
Hang on his breast the koko-tangiwai
Of glistening lucent jade.

Oh, thou wert the main prop of the house.
At the prow of our canoe thou stoodst,
Ears bent to the splashing sound
Of many paddles.

Our sweetest speaking-bird has gone,
The plumes alone remain.

—Old Maori lament

THERE is still a little while to go before school reopens after the summer holidays and quite a while yet before Mumma comes home . . . Rose and May write that when they visited Mumma they found her calm and pale and that she had lost a lot of weight. The blooms of the foxgloves ascending in bunches up the stalks all summer have moved over the tips to nothing and there are only spikes left selling millions of ripening seedboxes. But where are the vivid red and white of the last six months?

Where, for that matter, are a few other things? Where is that classic of a landlord character overplaying his role? He's stopped playing this role and has reverted to himself, for even a landlord has a conscience, and the part he played in Mrs. Considine's tragedy he claims he did not mean. But Hamish says it was the terror of the English curses Puppa laid upon him and his descendants in such colorful language;

whatever the reason he sledged back Mumma's elo-
quent wood the very next morning at daybreak after
she had been taken away, and, believe it or not, often
chops it himself. Which is the beginning of a new era
. . . or rather the recovery of the old era in London
when Harry Dunn was one of the Considine servants
and devoted to Richmond Considine. For now he
comes to the clearing to help, not hurt him. But that's
what life is . . . change.

And where is that guest that hung over Puppa's
windowsill from whom he allowed the children to take
money and after whose visits he smoked so furiously
and pronounced epigrams on the character of bore-
dom? She has returned to This Side House for reasons
exclusively her own. On her posh luggage Togi's wife,
one of the cooks there, reads the name "J. Eglantine,"
on Flower's tongue at the clearing you hear "Susianna
from Indiana," but at the end of a letter at the bottom
of the black box at the foot of Puppa's bed, written
years and *years* ago, is the slight word, "Jenny."

Miss Eglantine leans on the sill beneath the puriri
tree late one afternoon. She holds a white hat in her
hand and there's a jewel in her sunset hair. She's a
woman at the highest potential of beauty, which is
during the late thirties. Rose Considine in her white
uniform, whipping up and down the wards of the big
hospital in Auckland with that wonderful walk nurses
achieve, says that a woman should put her head in a

192

gas oven on the morning of her thirtieth birthday, but that's how it looks from twenty.

Which is not the only philosophy coming from Rose. When Sue asked her one day, "Why does Mumma punch poor Puppa?" she replied, "Because she thinks he does not love her. You should always punch a man if you think he doesn't love you. I've punched several so far."

"Does that make them love you?" from Huia.

"Rather," from Rose.

"And what happens then, Rose?"

"I drop them. I no longer want them."

Which is the failure in Jenny Eglantine's technique: she doesn't *punch* Puppa. She simply can't bring herself to do it, although devoutly believing it should be done. All she does is swear at him, which, as a gesture, barely gets through. Even her beauty won't work—not on its own, I mean. At this moment she is finding this out.

The valley is a place of magnificent pauses, strewn profligately like flowers on the roadside. Puppa fills his pipe and lights it taking all the time that's available in This Side and helping himself to the silence. At length he looks out over the foxglove spikes with not a bloom upon them. "They have been beautiful," he states.

"They're not now." Her voice has a low-running quality like a hidden stream in the night.

"No. They're not beautiful now. They're wonderful." A puff of smoke agrees.

Eyes as blue as a roadside daisy turn wonderingly upon the clearing. Through apertures in the foliage above her the sun probes with his sensitive fingers to this fine head he discovers here, not to mention this expensive sapphire set in a cloud of gold hair. He supposes it is some new kind of bloom and examines it tenderly, inspiring it to flashing life.

Over on the western rim, however, the rain mat appears, plainly with the intention of spreading across, while a finger of sunlight points to the presence of powdery rain in the air. With both the rain and the sun at hand, soon Tane Mahuta will fling his rainbow girdle from one end of the range to the other.

A lyrical bucolic scene straight out of an evening story together with what could have been a fairytale relationship—since it is only in stories that an early love returns to one's windowsill looking earlier and lovelier than ever—had it not been for this particular heroine's incurable, regrettable reality. Poor beautiful rational Jenny soberly discusses dispensables like "the past" and "the future" as if these were normal and relevant: What-you-said-then-you-bugger, what-I-said . . . from the frayed yellowed pages of yesteryear, the fungus of yesterlove . . . and what-you-promised-you-blasted-liar, what-you-should-do-you-damned-backslider and what-the-bloody-hell's-going-to-happen-to-me sort of thing in the so far unwritten future. All sincerely enough too as though these non sequiturs had a place in the clearing, indeed, as if they mattered. Whereas who in the clearing, let alone Richmond, can accommodate honest reason?

How could anyone from the factual outside world, even anyone as bewitching as Jenny, know that to This Side reality is unacceptable and seldom used as a workable fact; that the blood of the entire valley is bright-sparkling with silver corpuscles of fantasy, mercurial fantasy quite un-pin-downable by the fingertip of reality, quite undirectable by the cold winds of reason. Did anyone abiding here, inhabitant or guest, ever witness a yellow leaf blown from a poplar by any sort of air movement, let alone *wind*? They sit here on the trees during the motionless autumns like galaxies of candle flames, drifting to the ground exactly when they choose, not a moment before or after, to the pool of gold awaiting. Shimmery-still the air with dream, iridescent with the utterly unutterable impossible. Even rainstorms arrive under their own power directed by no more than the merest whim from some idling god above.

Poor little Jenny Eglantine with her line of thought. *Logic* . . . imagine it! in the valley of This Side. Later on when from far over the tops of the ranges the rain is preparing a studied entrance "Susianna from Indiana" is crying. But only Déodonné on

Puppa's knee and Clarendon at his knee appear to take note of it. What's new about crying in the clearing? Unless the tui in the rata vine nearby has a feeling for tears, which is rather unlikely; for some time now he has been looking this way but only at the jewel in the hair, thinking it some new kind of berry.

Puppa is studying the hole in the floor as he does when he's embarrassed, and into the silence comes the shod tread of Harry Dunn's feet in the back door, and the sound of the ax dropped in the corner. Yet even though he thumps into the kitchen and blurts, "I've done ya some wood, master," and goes again, Puppa still examines the hole in the floor.

Jenny, who is learning a thing or two by now, paces out from the tree, snatches a foxglove spike and snaps it. "Honestly, I mean to say . . . you haven't answered me once directly. You talk in the third person as though I were not here. You haven't answered me *at all*. Honestly, Richmond."

"God damn it, you interrupt."

"I don't care a damn." She snaps the remainder of the stalk. "What the bloody hell have I ever been to you *but* an interruption?" Very blue tears indeed. Clarendon and baby think they're lovely. They tip out and over upon her face like those of the mother in Puppa's stories except that those fell on someone else.

"Confound it, must you be specific?"

"Look, Richmond, you give me Trelawny. He's just like you. He's got your beautiful face and that exquisite coloring. I know why he cries all the time—his bawling is a preparation for shouting like yours. *I'd* know how to bring him up. I could do it standing on my head. It's a piece of cake. Honestly, Richmond, can't you see it? You said last week that a woman's tears should fall on someone else—let mine fall on him. They've fallen on you long enough, you bastard, and about you too for longer. Trelawny *should* have been my son. Had you married me I'd have had a son. You owe me a son, you bloody traitor." Fingers tearing at the pretty white hat. "I know why I'm crying all the time—you never gave me the son you owe me. Honestly, Richmond, I mean to say . . ."

"God almighty, where are my crutches?"

"Oh, look here, Richmond, you're a *meanie*. It's because of *you* I've had no one else's." It is much like the river lapping higher. "At the time I should have married I was gone on you. It's because of you I've got no son. You, you, *you* . . . Where is my son, my son?"

"Oh God, must I endure this? Why must everyone I meet enrage me? Clarendon, find my crutches."

"No, Puppa."

"Get off my knee and find my crutches."

"No, Puppa. Clarrie like lady."

"Like 'ady," from baby.

"See? You won't give me Trelawny, you bloody meanie. All those children and you can't spare one, not even the one you owe me. You said I was selfish but what about you? Talk about *selfish* . . . honestly, I mean to say . . . hundreds and *hundreds* of children you've got and you won't spare me *one*. Sitting here talking about f-foxgloves and—and f-fusion and s-states of mind. Talk doesn't produce a child. You *cra-a-azy* Considine. You know you love me. Honestly now, Richmond—I mean . . ."

"Daniel, Hamish, Rose, God damn it . . ."

"May, Flower, Susanna, God curse it. I know that off by heart. Just say you love me and I'll go. Richmond, honestly, I mean . . ."

Beyond the clearing upon the forest there's a soft rushing sound—the sound of approaching rain on the foliage making a personal entrance. Momentarily it remains so, increasing a little in volume. Now it reaches the nearer trees and the rushing is joined by a pattering. A moment or two of rushing and pattering till it strides across the clearing—rushing, pattering, chattering and all of a sudden a mighty clattering as the visitor pounds the roof. A fine, though studied, entrance.

"Richmond, honestly, I mean to say . . ." from beneath the tree.

A startling flash of lightning and both children

198

cower. It lights the whole of the humble room and the defenseless three within it; shows up esoteric recesses of the tree that knows no light so that you see the branch where the tui perches and the cuckoo's secret eyrie, and in the clearing you see the solitary tree fern separated from its mate.

"You've only got to say you love me."

The voice of the thunder god crashes all over. Cracks. Splits. Shatters. Appalls. The babies both cling to their father. A flock of birds takes off from the trees in swift mad intention. Where are the silly things heading? Do they suppose in their feathery minds that they can escape? They should cling to Tane, the forest father.

"Clarendon," from Puppa, "where are the children? Huia is afraid of thunder."

"Richmond, honestly . . . I mean to say . . ." Look at the pretty hair all spoilt and at the rain mixed up in her tears. Look at the sky-blue blouse all wet and the skirt she paid so much for, all to come to Richmond. The storm upon a woman. Won't he ask her inside or is she no more than a forest creature squealing at the vengeance of nature? "Richmond, remember those dawns together when we pledged each other forever. Honestly now, Richmond . . ."

"How enthralling the rain, magnificent the tempest. How royal is the thunder. By the living God, if I could walk I'd plunge into it unclothed." Grand he'd stride in the storm. It is like his life with Mary. It is his life with Mary.

Head on the sill, hat underfoot, blue blouse wringing with rain. "Honestly, Richmond . . ."

Another sound under the storm, a soft complex full thudding like distant galloping. He strains through the rain curtain with his single eye. It is a splashing and splattering now as the children in single file skim down the path. Pushing on the door, crowding through the porch, and here is the kitchen aloud with them, puffing, dripping, chaotic. "The god of the thunder, Puppa."

"Honestly . . ."

Y<small>ES</small> . . . it is someone singing.

Now where does this voice come from? It rises from somewhere down by the water . . . ah, there he is. It's that silly slave-born Memory with someone else's guitar, not his own, of course. But who wouldn't sing on a morning like this with the red of the rata inverted in the water, not a shiver in the reflections. Nothing of the picture in the river—except the ducks above— nothing in it moves.

Sire, another of Mai's "adopteds," is sitting with him, supplying the obbligato. Sire is divinely handsome and built like a god. He has the nobility of countenance of one whose head must be full of heavenly problems. No illustrious personage from the tenth heaven could easily better the profile. All that is missing is lightning flashing from his armpits and a gossamer rainbow girdle. Yet he too is a slave.

The song they are singing goes like this:

If I were a bird flying
I would fly right to your nest.
I would embrace your body
And you would turn to me . . .
You would turn to me.

From Togi on the deck, "Hey, you fulla, you shake
up a leg and get these luggage on board."

Though is sleeping your body [continues the song]
Is walking your spirit,
Is sighing your heart,
And you turn to me . . .
You turn to me.

"You two helluva guys. You shake your guts. Get
these luggage on board."

Give me your love
To hold in my hands.
My desire is overflowing.
Turn to me, oh,
Turn to me.

A coil of rope lands smack between them, thrown
from the deck, and the two of them turn to the boat
instead.

202

All sorts of smart bags are carted precariously over one single plank from the landing to the deck that Togi is pleased to call his gangway: the most elegant suitcases of the guests who have completed their stay in This Side and who will be down here in person shortly. But what are Memory and Sire to make of these sacks and sacks of useless funguses piled up on the jetty? "Sling 'em on," from Togi. "One of these gues' she crazy enough to take it away and sell it. I knows where we sell it. We sell it to my brother the taniwha. We chuck it overboard to him later down-river. Somehow we got to fool these kid."

Down-river later, true enough, all this fungus gathered over years and years by the children in the forest to buy Puppa a wheelchair does get chucked overboard to the taniwha, not without a word to the guest concerned. "That's what I meant in the first place," she says. She has on a large heavy overcoat although the morning is hot. "It's not so much the wheelchair I'm thinking of, Captain. It's the children. I don't want them to suffer their faith wrecked so early," a tear, "as mine has been wrecked so late."

In the deep slow water of a gorge down-river where the whole lot goes overboard the taniwha is not impressed. He doesn't know what to make of the stuff. Surely they know he's only interested in souls for food. Is there a soul in this disorderly substance? He decides to leave it for the eels. As for the eels they're puzzled, revolted, and they reject it too. It sinks among the boulders at the bottom.

One very early morning, as summer is at last faltering, before the Dawn Maid peers over the eastern horizon, as the birds are still thinking about clearing their throats for the usual dawn chorus another sound arises. It is a human voice and it comes from That Side. It's the voice of the kuia, Niki. It begins sepulchrally on a low note as she walks out from the ancient dwelling place into the pre-dawn darkness; it rises, rises, gathering in volume till it reaches the top of the throat. And its message flies across-river like an urgent bird to the landing and then to the store, hurries barefoot as far as the lindens and across the road to the House. From there it beats on puffing breath as far as This Side pa and from there to the rest of the village. "The old one is dead. He died before dawn this morning. He died in the dwelling place on That Side. Huia was there." So that by the time the Dawn Maid arrives and the chorus is in full swing, everyone in This Side knows.

During the week of the mighty tangi with Maoris flocking from up-, down- and across-river, from Raetihi and Whanganui, from coast to coast of the North Island and even from the very tip where departing spirits leave for Hawaiki, with the haka and poi teams practicing in climactic concentration for the post-burial entertainment functions . . . Huia is surprised and impressed rather than sorrowed to find the old one not lying in his rugs in the dwelling place but heroic in a shiny new coffin with gleaming silver handles brought up in the boat some time ago. Moreover he doesn't try to teach her anything now, least of all her own genealogy.

And she is surprised that his eyes remain closed, withdrawing for all time the benignity in one, the malignity in the other, but he looks more like a chief this way, more representative of all the culture he has taught her. For one thing his impressive tattooing shows up on the blood-drained skin, and for another he's officially clothed. There's a feather of the extinct huia bird in his hair, there are precious jewel-stones in his ears and on his breast is the koko-tangiwai of glistening lucent greenstone. As for his cloak of kiwi feathers, it is no less than the famous Taharangi. For the first time to her he looks a rangatira.

No one can say Huia is upset. There is something between a child and a grandparent that is not between a child and a great-grandparent. There was no evidence that the old one had for Huia much more than an interest in her as a descendant of tribal importance or that she had felt other than such toward him. It was his granddaughter, Huia's mother, Kaa, whom the old one had loved even more than his daughter Whai—as it is with Huia: it is Daniel's father rather than Daniel himself who evokes this something, this inexplicable affinity.

To Huia during these days of the week-long tangi there is a certain confusion; there is without doubt a new attitude among the tribe toward her although she is unable to define it. She tries to work her way through it all to find her new footing, to track down her responsibility. She's a girl of eleven or twelve, they think, but surely not thirteen, by no means too young for it. There's no substitute for the new rangatira whatever her age.

She does manage to pin down the fact, however, that whereas she was the one to approach the others it is now they who approach her. Casually enough. She notices that it is the notorious Tohunga Makutu who takes her aside rather than she who engages him. This Tohunga Makutu is the acknowledged subvillain of This Side and the intimate, they say, of the true villain, the taniwha in the river, the deep subconscious of the valley mind. It is he who is responsible for most of the makutu in the valley, including the effective one on the clearing. Yet he's the most charming person to meet. He is not thin and spiritual like her koro but frankly fat and practical, he speaks the most accurate English when he chooses and also cultivated Maori, and his smile is the thing about him. He has a

magnetism of personality that draws one and all including the taniwha. But not a soul in the valley trusts
him and all swear they will never attend his tangi
should that blessed day ever come. He's a man round
about the sixties.

Yet this man knew the grand passion: it was Whai
Te Renga Renga and it was his failure with her that
bred his vengeance and turned him to makutu.

Death by limb-withering to avenge Whai Te Renga
    Renga.
Death at childbirth to avenge Whai Te Renga Renga.
Death, death . . . ah . . .

He tells the new rangatira now as they stand beneath the carvings, "If were limb-withered or brought
to the death mat many, many of the white race, yet
would not be avenged for me Whai Te Renga Renga."

In Maori from Huia, "You forget, O Tohunga, my
own white blood."

"Hate I the desecration of the white man."

"What does desecration mean?"

"Desecration means 'to insult the tapu.' "

"When I am older I'll be able to answer you better,
O Tohunga. At the moment all is confusion. Much to
be said is there on this subject."

By the end of the week when the time comes to
send the spirit of the old one to Hawaiki it is old Niki

who clothes the new rangatira in the ceremonial cloak to speak the last lament and who places in her ears the precious jewel-stones. But she has spent the entire morning trying to comb Huia's hair as Huia watches the grave being finished off beside her mother, Kaa, beneath the towering poplar. This black hair reaches to her waist by now, thick and luminous, like a stream of water. When at last old Niki is satisfied with it and not one strand strays from its place, she fixes a taniko band round her head, low across the forehead above the brows, and in it places the huia feather, the symbol of her rank. The traditional flax piupiu is, of course, too big for her, wraps round her waist twice and reaches below the calves of her legs, while the ceremonial cloak of kiwi touches the ground in places. Yet as she stands with the sun on her head and the reflections in her eyes, barefoot before the bier, she is indisputably a rangatira. Neither does her childish voice stumble at any phrase as she chants the final lament:

Depart, O my koro, to greet your weaponed ancestors.
Depart, O Rangatira, to join your illustrious ancestors.

In your hair the huia plume,
On your breast the greenstone Kahurangi,
Upon you a fine flaxen cloak and
Stately are you to look upon.

208

At the coming, with high and decorated prow,
Your last canoe,
Take now your paddle named Kautu-ki-te-rangi
And ply across the tide to your far home,
Hawaiki.

O descendant of great ancestors,
Take your paddle.
O descendant of mighty warriors,
Depart.
Gaze thou upon your weaponed ancestors.

S O THERE y'are, y'see," from Mumma leaning back in her chair with palms upturned. "That's y'makutu for you. That's what it did to me." She is slim now and white of face, her hands are soft and she wears a pretty dress and shoes. May it was who bought the dress which is patterned with flowers like those of the guests who loiter beneath the lindens and laugh out loud on the river, and it was Rose who bought her the white shoes. She is so brand-new that the children to a man keep their distance, outrageously shy. Her gray eyes lift to Puppa at his end of the table, "Well, Richie . . . d'you think that too? That it's time we got away from these curses?"

"Daniel and Hamish have completed the purchase of a magnificent house for us. In the city of Tauranga by the sea."

"Ay? What's that, what's that? What did y'say? Have they got the title deeds?"

210

"Balconies and balustrades," in the voice of story, "at least two staircases and a rose garden at the front. There's a long drive through the trees, they write, and sonorous seas surrounding. There's not a curse of any kind chanted upon that house, there's only a blessing on it. We shall live happily ever after."

"Ay? Is it true? Is it true? D'you expect me to believe a miracle?"

"Miracles occur every day."

"What's that you say, Richie? Miracles happen every day?"

"This is one fine story that is coming true, along with a few of the others. No doubt I will walk again over there . . . the climate, you know, Mary."

"They won't get us there. Aha, aha—that'll teach them."

"Teach who, Mumma?"

"All the dreadful people in this place. This is *one* for them all."

"One for they's all," from Clarendon.

"Ha-ha, ha-ha-ha. It won't get us there. The makutu won't get us there. Ay, Richie, ay? *Ha-a-a* . . . it won't get us there."

"Who tat lady?" from Clarendon.

"Tat ady?" from Déodonné.

A shriek of staccato laughter from Mumma and a chorus from them all.

"That's our mother," from Simon.

From Mumma, "To think they don't recognize me. My own babies and they don't know their mother." A sigh and she turns to the window. "Open the window, someone, please. I need fresh air. And open the door, Simon."

Puppa, "You always want to look out for miracles. They happen every day."

Mumma, "We'll make the tea on that, shall we, Richie?"

Huia, "I'll bring in some wood."

They leave the old piano here and the rest of the token furniture. They would have taken their books, had they ever had any, but there never had been any books; not written books, I mean. They don't even take Puppa's black box at the foot of his bed in the kitchen. "I don't choose to take the past with me," is all he utters on that. "Let the spiders have it. Those manuscripts will improve their minds and possibly their webs too; they'll provide a certain perspective missing in this place. An opossum or rabbit can read those pages to the ferrets, stoats and weasels. Some academic owl can take my place—or some other forest creature."

From Huia, "I'll read to them, Puppa. I'm a forest creature."

Togi, with Memory and Sire, have to nail three

whole planks together to get Puppa on the boat, carrying him over between them. But when the Considines take off down-river on the last morning of summer they leave one of their name behind them; Huia Brice Considine stands on the landing holding with both hands her greenstone.

The broad major chords of summer are graduating into the minor; maybe there will be winter after all.

Yet thousand-jacket still blooms on the bluff where Tikawe's bones are resting, while in the drawing room of This Side House it stands breast-high in the containers, yet at the base of the spikes of tiny blossoms many have disrobed; their nectar is sucked, their fragrance dead, their seed-wombs are swelling and their purpose fulfilled. For them at least the summer is over.

The seeds of the foxgloves in the clearing have already scattered. No more beat of red and white, no more the thrill of rising wombs; the gaunt stalks accuse the heavens. Only emptiness they know for the moment; the emptiness, the starkness and the agony from a moment of rapture over.

Autumn overlaps summer but summer has to end sometime. Nothing can stop the colossal-scale sequence of the seasons under way in This Side . . . the coloring, seeding and fruiting. No human heart can hope to halt the tremendous momentum of it. No crying or laughter, no tragedy or joy can stay the pounding moments. They are born like flowers, they swell to fulfillment, they wither and they die. One by one they come and go: this one, that one; this one, that one; this, that; this, that . . . tick-tock, tick-tock. A minute comes and goes, a day comes and goes, a season comes and goes, a year comes and goes, and even though at the climax of summer the before and the after are forgotten inevitably the descent sets in and autumn leads down to winter.

As a being emerging from the blindness of fusion once more remembers the past and recovers doubt of the future, his spirit once again beginning to fall from the gods' tenth heaven to hell, summer once more gives way to autumn as the year in This Side turns over.

Maori Words

ANA: Yes

AO: Light

AROHA: Love

AUE: Expression of distress

HAKA: A dance with words

HAWAIKI: The unknown spot on the earth's surface where the Maoris claim to have come from, and to which their spirits will return

HUIA: A native bird, now believed extinct, whose tail feathers were greatly prized by the Maoris as a mark of rank

HUKARERE: An historic, Maori girls' college

KAA: Fire, burn

KAITEKE: Flax cloak

KARAKIA: Incantation

KAUTU-KI-TE-RANGI: The name of one of the steering paddles of the Aotea canoe which came to New Zealand with the fleet of seven canoes in the Great Migration of the fourteenth century

KIWI: A native bird, wingless, whose feathers the Maoris used for cloaks of rank

KORO: Old man

KOROWAI: A cloak of dressed flax decorated with feathers

215

KOWHAI: A native tree with golden blossoms, New Zealand's emblem flower

KUIA: Old woman

KUMARA: Sweet potato

MAKUTU: Black magic

MANUKA: A wild bush with delicate white flowers

MARAE: The area before a meeting house where tribal discussions take place

MERE: A skull-splitter made of greenstone or whalebone

MOKOPUNA: Grandchild

NGATI: Tribe

PA: Maori village

PAKEHA: White person

PAPA: The earth

PIUPIU: Skirt made of flax leaves

PO: Night, darkness

POI: A hand dance with a small flax ball on a string swung and twirled rhythmically to a song; also, the ball itself

PUHI: Virgin

RANGATIRA: Chief, chieftainness

RANGI: Sky

RORO: Porch of a meeting house

TAIAHA: Carved wooden spear

TAKARANGI: Name of a famous greenstone

TAKU: My

TANE MAHUTA: God of the forest

TANGI: Weep, funeral

TANIKO: A woven design in flax fiber

TANIWHA: Water monster

TAPU: Sacred; a spiritual ban

TE AUTE: An historic Maori boys' college

TE ROKO-O-WHITI: The name of the other steering paddle of the Aotea canoe

TIKI: A grotesque carving of a man

TOHUNGA: Priest

TOHUNGA MAKUTU: A priest who uses his supernatural powers for the purposes of evil

TUI: The emblem bird of New Zealand

WAIATA: Maori song

WHARE: Very small house